Michael Moorcock has already told some of the earlier adventures of Corum Jhaelen Irsei in *The Books of Corum*. *The Oak and the Ram* follows *The Bull and the Spear* (also in Quartet paperbacks) in a new series, *The Chronicles of Prince Corum and The Silver Hand*, and will be followed by *The Sword and the Stallion*.

'Like Tolkien and Roger Zelazny, Moorcock has the ability to create a wholly imaginative world landscaped with vivid and sometimes frightening reality, and peopled with magicians, heroes and monsters who are far from the one-dimensional creatures of fairy tales but who possess human warmth and interaction . . . bargains, symbols, rituals and vicious battles enliven a glittering story as Corum embarks on another heroic quest' – *The Times*

'One of the best fantasy writers in the language' – *Tribune*

THE OAK AND THE RAM

Volume the Second of
*The Chronicle of Prince Corum
and The Silver Hand*

Q _____

MICHAEL MOORCOCK

QUARTET BOOKS   LONDON

Published by Quartet Books Limited 1974
27 Goodge Street, London W1P 1FD

First published by Allison and Busby Ltd 1973

Copyright © 1973 by Michael Moorcock

ISBN 0 704 31128 3

Printed in Great Britain by
Hunt Barnard Printing Ltd, Aylesbury, Bucks.

For Jarmila

PROLOGUE

In those days there were oceans of light and cities in the skies and wild flying beasts of bronze. There were herds of crimson cattle that roared and were taller than castles. There were shrill, viridian things that haunted bleak rivers. It was a time of gods, manifesting themselves upon our world in all her aspects; a time of giants who walked on water; of mindless sprites and misshapen creatures who could be summoned by an ill-considered thought but driven away only on pain of some fearful sacrifice; of magics, phantasms, unstable nature, impossible events, insane paradoxes, dreams come true, dreams gone awry; of nightmares assuming reality.

It was a rich time and a dark time. The time of the Sword Rulers. The time when the Vadhagh and the Nhadragh, age-old enemies, were dying. The time when Man, the slave of fear, was emerging, unaware that much of the terror he experienced was the result of nothing else but the fact that he, himself, had come into existence. It was one of many ironies connected with Man (who, in those days, called his race Mabden).

The Mabden lived brief lives and bred prodigiously. Within a few centuries they rose to dominate the westerly continent on which they had evolved. Superstition stopped them from sending many of their ships towards Vadhagh and Nhadragh lands for another century or two, but gradually they gained courage when no resistance was offered. They began to feel jealous of

1

the older races; they began to feel malicious.

The Vadhagh and the Nhadragh were not aware of this. They had dwelt a million or more years upon the planet which now, at last, seemed at rest. They knew of the Mabden, but considered them not greatly different from other beasts. Though continuing to indulge their traditional hatreds of one another, the Vadhagh and the Nhadragh spent their long hours in considering abstractions, in the creation of works of art and the like. Rational, sophisticated, at one with themselves, these older races were unable to believe in the changes that had come. Thus, as it almost always is, they ignored the signs.

There was no exchange of knowledge between the two ancient enemies, even though they had fought their last battle many centuries before.

The Vadhagh lived in family groups occupying isolated castles scattered across a continent called by them Bro-an-Vadhagh. There was scarcely any communication between these families, for the Vadhagh had long since lost the impulse to travel. The Nhadragh lived in their cities built on the islands in the seas to the northwest of Bro-an-Vadhagh. They, also, had little contact, even with their closest kin. Both races reckoned themselves invulnerable. Both were wrong.

Upstart Man was beginning to breed and spread like a pestilence across the world. This pestilence struck down the old races wherever it touched them. And it was not only death that Man brought, but terror, too. Wilfully, he made of the older world nothing but ruins and bones. Unwittingly, he brought psychic and supernatural disruption of a magnitude which even the Great Old Gods failed to comprehend.

And the Great Old Gods began to know fear.

And Man, slave of fear, arrogant in his ignorance, continued his stumbling progress. He was blind to the huge disruptions aroused by his apparently petty ambitions. As well, Man was deficient in sensitivity, had no awareness of the multitude of dimensions that filled the universe, each plane intersecting with several others. Not so the Vadhagh or the Nhadragh, who had known what it was to move at will between the dimensions they termed the Five Planes. They had glimpsed and understood the nature of many planes, other than the Five, through which the Earth moved.

Therefore it seemed a dreadful injustice that these wise races should perish at the hands of creatures who were still little more than animals. It was as if vultures feasted on and

2

squabbled over the paralysed body of the youthful poet who could only stare at them with puzzled eyes as they slowly robbed him of an exquisite existence they would never appreciate, never know they were taking.

'If they valued what they stole, if they knew what they were destroying,' says the old Vadhagh in the story, 'The Only Autumn Flower', 'then I would be consoled.'

It was unjust.

By creating Man, the universe had betrayed the old races.

But it was a perpetual and familiar injustice. The sentient may perceive and love the universe, but the universe cannot perceive and love the sentient. The universe sees no distinction between the multitude of creatures and elements which comprise it. All are equal. None is favoured. The universe, equipped with nothing but the materials and the power of creation, continues to create: something of this, something of that. It cannot control what it creates and it cannot, it seems, be controlled by its creations (though a few might deceive themselves otherwise). Those who curse the workings of the universe curse that which is deaf. Those who strike out at those workings fight that which is inviolate. Those who shake their fists, shake their fists at blind stars.

But this does not mean there are not some who will try to do battle with and destroy the invulnerable. There will always be such beings, sometimes beings of great wisdom, who cannot bear to believe in an insouciant universe.

Prince Corum Jhaelen Irsei was one of these. Perhaps the last of the Vadhagh race, he was sometimes known as the Prince in the Scarlet Robe.

This is the second chronicle concerning his adventures. The first chronicle, known as 'The Books of Corum', told how the Mabden followers of Earl Glandyth-a-Krae killed Prince Corum's relatives and his nearest kin and thus taught the Prince in the Scarlet Robe how to hate, how to kill, and how to desire vengeance. We have heard how Earl Glandyth tortured Prince Corum and took away a hand and an eye and how Corum was rescued by the Giant of Laahr and taken to the castle of the Margravine Rhalina – a castle set upon a mount surrounded by the sea. Though Rhalina was a Mabden woman (of the gentler folk of Lwym-an-Esh), Corum and she fell in love. When Glandyth roused the Pony Tribes, the forest barbarians, to attack the Margravine's castle, she and Corum sought supernatural aid and thus fell into the hands of the

3

sorcerer Shool, whose domain was the island called Svi-an-Fanla-Brool – Home of the Gorged God. And now Corum had direct experience of the morbid, unfamiliar powers at work in the world. Shool spoke of dreams and realities ('I see you are beginning to argue in Mabden terms,' he told Corum. 'It is just as well for you, if you wish to survive in this Mabden dream.' – 'It is a dream . . . ?' said Corum. – 'Of sorts. Real enough. It is what you might call the dream of a God. Then again you might say that it is a dream that a God has allowed to become reality. I refer of course to the Knight of the Swords, who rules the Five Planes . . . ').

With Rhalina his prisoner, Shool could make a bargain with Corum. He gave him two gifts – the Hand of Kwll and the Eye of Rhynn – to replace his own missing organs. These jewelled and alien things were once the property of two brother gods known as the Lost Gods since they mysteriously vanished.

Armed with these Corum began his great quest, which was to take him against all three Sword Rulers – the Knight, the Queen and the King of the Swords – the mighty Lords of Chaos. And Corum discovered much concerning these gods, the nature of reality and the nature of his own identity. He learned that he was the Champion Eternal, that, in a thousand other guises, in a thousand other ages, it was his lot to struggle against those forces which attacked reason, logic and justice, no matter what form they took. And, at long last, he was able to overwhelm (with the help of a mysterious ally) those forces and banish gods from his world.

Peace came to Bro-an-Vadhagh and Corum took his mortal bride to his ancient castle which stood on a cliff overlooking a bay. And meanwhile the few surviving Vadhagh and Nhad-ragh turned again to their own devices, and the golden land of Lwym-an-Esh flourished and became the centre of the Mabden world – famous for its scholars, its bards, its artists, its builders and its warriors. A great age dawned for the Mabden folk; they flourished. And Corum was pleased that his wife's folk flourished. On the few occasions when Mabden travellers passed near Castle Erorn he would feast them well and be filled with gladness when he heard of the beauties of Halwyg-nan-Vake, capital city of Lwym-an-Esh, whose walls bloomed with flowers all year round. And the travellers would tell Corum and Rhalina of the new ships which brought great prosperity to the land, so that none of Lwym-an-Esh knew hunger. They would tell of the new laws which gave all a voice in the affairs of that country. And Corum listened and was proud of Rhalina's race.

To one such traveller he offered an opinion: 'When the last of the Vadhagh and the Nhadragh have disappeared from this world,' he said, 'the Mabden will emerge as a greater race than ever were we.'

'But we shall never have your powers of sorcery,' answered the traveller, and he caused Corum to laugh heartily.

'We had no sorcery at all! We had no conception of it. Our "sorcery" was merely our observation and manipulation of certain natural laws, as well as our perception of other planes of the multiverse, which we have now all but lost. It is the Mabden who imagine such things as sorcery – who would always rather invent the miraculous than investigate the ordinary (and find the miraculous therein). Such imaginations will make your race the most exceptional this Earth has yet known, but those imaginations could also destroy you!'

'Did we invent the Sword Rulers whom you so heroically fought?'

'Aye,' answered Corum, 'I suspect that you did! And I suspect that you might invent others again.'

'Invent phantoms? Fabulous beasts? Powerful gods? Whole cosmologies?' said the astonished traveller. 'Are all these things, then, unreal?'

'They're real enough,' Corum replied. 'Reality, after all, is the easiest thing in the world to create. It is partly a question of need, partly a question of time, partly a question of circumstance . . . '

Corum had felt sorry for confounding his guest and he laughed again and passed on to other topics.

And so the years went by and Rhalina began to show signs of age while Corum, near-immortal, showed none. Yet still they loved each other – perhaps with greater intensity as they realised that the day drew near when death would part her from him.

Their life was sweet; their love was strong. They needed little but each other's company.

And then she died.

And Corum mourned for her. He mourned without the sadness which mortals have (which is, in part, sadness for themselves and fear of their own death).

Some seventy years had passed since the Sword Rulers fell,

and the travellers grew fewer and fewer as Corum of the Vadhagh people became more of a legend in Lwym-an-Esh than he was remembered as a creature of ordinary flesh. He had been amused when he had heard that in some country parts of that land there were now shrines to him and crude images of him to which folk prayed as they had prayed to their gods. It had not taken them long to find new gods and it was ironic that they should make one of the person who had helped rid them of their old ones. They magnified his feats and, in so doing, simplified him as an individual. They attributed magical powers to him; they told stories of him which they had once told of their previous gods. Why was the truth never enough for the Mabden? Why must they forever embellish and obscure it? What a paradoxical people they were!

Corum recalled his parting with his friend, Jhary-a-Conel, self-styled Companion to Champions, and the last words he had spoken to him – 'New gods can always be created,' he had said. Yet he had never guessed, then, from what at least one of those gods would be created.

And, because he had become divine to so many, the people of Lwym-an-Esh took to avoiding the headland on which stood ancient Castle Erorn, for they knew that gods had no time to listen to the silly talk of mortals.

Thus Corum grew lonelier still; he became reluctant to travel in Mabden lands, for this attitude of the folk made him uncomfortable.

In Lwym-an-Esh those who had known him well, known that, save for his longer lifespan he was as vulnerable as themselves, were now all dead, too. So there were none to deny the legends.

And, likewise, because he had grown used to Mabden ways and Mabden people about him, he found that he could not find much pleasure in the company of his own race, for they retained their remoteness, their inability to understand their situation, and would continue to do so until the Vadhagh race perished for good. Corum envied them their lack of concern, for, though he took no part in the affairs of the world, he still felt involved enough to speculate about the possible destiny of the various races.

A kind of chess, which the Vadhagh played, took up much of his time (he played against himself, using the pieces like arguments, testing one strain of logic against another). Brooding upon his various past conflicts, he doubted, sometimes, if they had ever taken place at all. He wondered if the portals to the fifteen planes were closed forever now, even to the Vadhagh and the Nhadragh, who had once moved in and out of them so freely. If this were so, did it mean that, effectively, those other planes no longer existed? And thus his dangers, his fears, his discoveries, slowly took on the quality of little more than abstractions; they became factors in an argument concerning the nature of time and identity and, after a while, the argument itself ceased to interest Corum.

Some eighty years were to pass since the fall of the Sword Rulers before Corum's interest was to be re-awakened in matters concerning the Mabden folk and their gods.

And this interest was awakened in a strange way when Corum heard voices in his dreams. The voices craved his help and called him a god, called him Corum Llaw Ereint – Corum of the Silver Hand. And Corum denied the voices until Jhary-a-Conel, his mysterious old friend who seemed able to cross between the planes at will, advised him to heed their call, for they were the descendants of Rhalina's own folk – the folk of Lwym-an-Esh. For Corum was the Champion Eternal and it was his fate to fight in all the great wars involving the most crucial and profound events in mankind's destiny.

So at last Corum agreed and he garbed himself in all the martial finery of the Vadhagh and he strapped on the best of his artificial silver hands (which could perform all the functions of a fleshly hand) and he went riding on a red horse into the future to meet the folk of Cremm Croich and to battle the horrible Fhoi Myore, the Gods of Limbo, the Cold Folk, the People of the Pines.

He found a world attacked by winter – a world fast freezing to death as the Fhoi Myore drew all heat from the land, wherever they conquered; and they poisoned whatever they conquered, without thought for their own existence, for they were moved by primal desires not by intelligence, and they desired death, And many had already perished of the Mabden folk and the treasures of the Mabden had been stolen or scattered and their Great Kings had been slain or captured or sent into hiding. And only a few small tribes in the remote west or in the distant north had not yet been in conflict with the Fhoi Myore – seven gods in seven crude wicker chariots drawn by seven foul beasts, seven gods who could destroy whole armies with a glance and whose leader was Kerenos who controlled a pack of hellish hounds.

7

From King Mannach of Caer Mahlod, from Medhbh, the king's daughter, Corum learned that only the Black Bull of Crinanass could drive off the Fhoi Myore in some unknown way. And the woman was fair, this Medhbh, and she was strong and a warrior and Corum was reminded of Rhalina, his dead love, and he was stirred by Medhbh.

He was told of his quest. His quest was to the land of Hy-Breasail, beyond the sea. This land was enchanted and no mortal returned from it. But Corum, they said, was a god, a Sidhi. He could go to Hy-Breasail.

And so he went. Through a winter world he went (though it was not winter-time) and had many adventures, encountered many strange folk, talked with wizards and with Sidhi, made bargains and heard a prophecy. An old woman warned him that he should fear a harp, a brother and beauty. Corum was puzzled by the prophecy and particularly puzzled as to why he should fear beauty. But he went on to Hy-Breasail, the only remaining part of sea-covered Lwym-an-Esh, and there he found the spear, Bryionak, one of the lost treasures of the Mabden which could, in the right hands, control the Black Bull. And many more adventures followed until he returned to Caer Mahlod as the Fhoi Myore attacked in all their dreadful might – seven malformed gods, together with their servants, the lost, the evil, the damned and the undying, led by Corum's old enemy Prince Gaynor, who could not be slain but yearned for death. And there was a battle at Caer Mahlod and the battle went ill for the Mabden until the Bull was summoned and drove off the Fhoi Myore's undead slaves and slew one of those crude, cruel gods and caused the others to flee.

Then took place the final rite and the land was made green again around Caer Mahlod and the Black Bull of Crinanass and the spear, Bryionak, were never again seen in mortal lands.

And Corum and Medhbh lay together in love, but still Corum brooded on the prophecy, for he knew he was the Champion Eternal and as doomed to struggle as was Prince Gaynor.

And the Fhoi Myore, the Lost Gods of Limbo, remained upon the Earth.

THE CHRONICLE OF CORUM AND THE SILVER HAND

Book One

In which Prince Corum finds
himself called to pursue the
second of his great quests . . .

1. THE MEETING
OF THE KINGS

And so Rhalina had died.

And Corum had found Medhbh, King Mannach's daughter, and in a short while (as Corum reckoned time) she too would die. If it was his weakness to fall in love with short-lived Mabden women, then he must reconcile himself to the knowledge that he would outlive many lovers, must experience many losses, many agonies. As it was, he did not think much about it, preferring to avoid the significance of such ideas whenever possible. Besides, the memories of Rhalina were growing dim and it was only with difficulty that he could remember the fine details of the life he had led in an earlier age than this, when he had ridden against the Sword Rulers.

Corum Jhaelen Irsei, who had been called the Prince in the Scarlet Robe (but, having since traded this robe to a wizard, was now know as Corum of the Silver Hand), stayed at Caer Mahlod for two months after the day when the Black Bull of Crinanass had run its fecund course and brought sudden spring to the land of the Tuha-na-Cremm Croich, the People of the Mound. It was two months since the misshaped Fhoi Myore had tried to slay the inhabitants of Caer Mahlod, to freeze and to poison this place so that it might, too, resemble Limbo from whence the Fhoi Myore came and to which they were unable to return.

Now the Fhoi Myore appeared to have abandoned their

ambitions of conquest. The Fhoi Myore were stranded upon this plane and had no love for its inhabitants, but they did not fight for the joy of fighting. The Fhoi Myore were only six. The Fhoi Myore had once been many. But the Fhoi Myore were dying of long-drawn-out diseases which would eventually rot them. In the meantime, however, they made themselves as comfortable as possible upon the Earth, turning the world into bleak and perpetual Samhain, a mid-winter world. And before the Fhoi Myore expired they would, casually, have destroyed the entire Mabden race as well.

But very few of the Mabden were in a mood to think about such a prospect. They had triumphed over the Fhoi Myore once and won their freedom. It seemed enough, for the summer was the richest and the hottest any remembered (some sweated and joked that they would welcome the return of the Cold Folk, they panted so much in the heat), as if the sun, giving no warmth to the rest of the Mabden lands, poured all its power into one small corner of the world.

The oaks were greener, the alders were stronger, the ash and the elms were the lushest they had ever been. In the fields there was wheat ripening where folk had never hoped to see another harvest.

There were poppies and cornflowers and marigolds, buttercups, woodbine, hollyhocks and daisies growing everywhere in profusion.

Only the cold, cold water pouring down in the rivers which flowed from the east reminded the folk of Tuha-na-Cremm Croich that their countrymen were all dead, or vassals of the Fhoi Myore, or both; that their High King – their Archdruid Amergin – was under a glamour, a prisoner in his own city at Caer Llud, a city now used as their capital by the Fhoi Myore. Only that reminded them, whenever they bent to drink. And many were made gloomy, brooding upon their incapacity to avenge their dead cousins, for the best they had done was defend their own land against the Cold Folk and even then they could not have accomplished the defence without the help of Sidhi magic and a demigod raised from his deep slumber beneath the Mound. That demigod was Corum.

The water flowed from the east and it fed the wide ditch they had dug around the conical mound on which was built the fortress city of Caer Mahlod, an old city, of grey and bulky granite; a city without much beauty but with considerable strength. Caer Mahlod had been abandoned at least once and re-occupied in times of war. It was the only city that remained to the Tuha-na-Cremm Croich. Once they had had several fairer cities, but these had been swept away by the ice which the Fhoi Myore brought.

But now many of those who had occupied the fortress town had returned to rebuild their ruined farms and tend the crops which had been revitalized by the Black Bull's life-blood and only King Mannach and King Mannach's warriors and retainers and King Mannach's daughter and Corum remained at Caer Mahlod.

Sometimes Corum would stand on the battlements and look towards the sea and the ruins of his own home, which was now called Castle Owyn and thought a natural formation, and wonder upon the matter of the spear Bryionak and the Black Bull and the magic which had been worked. It seemed to him that he dreamed, for he could not explain the magic or how it had been brought about. He dreamed the dream of these people, who had called him from a dream. And for the most part he was content. He had Medhbh of the Long Arm (the nickname she had earned for her skill with spear and tathlum), with her thick red hair, her strong beauty, her intelligence and her laughter. He had dignity. He had the respect of his fellow warriors. They had become used to him now. They accepted his strange Vadhagh looks – 'elfin' looks, Medhbh called them – his artificial silver hand, his single yellow and purple eye and the patch over the other socket; the patch embroidered by Rhalina, Margravine of Moidel's Mount, who lay a thousand years at least in the past.

He had dignity. He had been true to this folk and he had been true to himself. He had pride.

And he had fine companionship. There was no question that his lot was improved since he had left Castle Erorn and answered the call of this folk. He wondered what had become of Jhary-a-Conel, Companion to Heroes. It had been Jhary, after all, who had advised him to do King Mannach's bidding. But Jhary was the last mortal Corum knew who could still travel through the Fifteen Planes, apparently at will. Once all the Vadhagh could move between the planes, as could the Nhadragh, but with the defeat of the Sword Rulers the last vestiges of this power had been denied them.

And sometimes Corum would call a bard to him to sing one of the old songs of the Tuha-na-Cremm Croich, for he found such songs to his taste. One song was attributed to the

13

first Amergin, ancestor to the High King, now a thrall of the Fhoi Myore, upon arriving in their new homeland:

I am the ocean wave;
I am the murmur of the surges;
I am seven battalions;
I am a strong bull;
I am an eagle on a rock;
I am a ray of the sun;
I am the most beautiful of herbs;
I am a courageous wild boar;
I am a salmon in the water;
I am a lake upon a plain;
I am a cunning artist;
I am gigantic, sword-wielding champion;
I can shift my shape like a god.
In what direction shall we go?
Shall we hold our council in the valley or in the mountain-top?
Where shall we make our home?
What land is better than this island of the setting sun?
Where shall we walk to and fro in peace and safety?
Who can find you clear springs of water as can I?
Who can tell you the age of the moon but I?
Who can call the fish from the depths of the sea as can I?
Who can lure them near the shore as can I?
Who can change the shapes of the hills and the headlands as can I?
I am a bard who is called upon by seafarers to prophesy.
Javelins shall be wielded to avenge our wrongs.
I prophesy victory.
I end my song by prophesying all other good things.

And then the bard would sing his own song as a kind of amplification to Amergin's:

I have been in many shapes before I attained congenial form.
I have been a narrow blade of a sword;
I have been a drop in the air;
I have been a shining star;
I have been a word in a book;
I have been a book in the beginning;
I have been a light in a lantern a year and a half;
I have been a bridge for passing over three score rivers;

I have journeyed as an eagle;
I have been a boat on the sea;
I have been a director in battle;
I have been a sword in the hand;
I have been a shield in a fight;
I have been the string of a harp;
I have been enchanted for a year in the foam of water;
There is nothing in which I have not been.

And in these old songs Corum would hear echoes of his
own fate, which Jhary-a-Conel had explained to him – the
fate to be eternally reborn, sometimes fully grown, as a warrior
to fight in all the great battles of mortals, whether those mortals
be Mabden, Vadhagh or some other race; to fight for the
freedom of mortals oppressed by gods (for all that many believed the gods created *by* mortals). In those songs he heard
an expression of the dreams he sometimes had – where he was
the whole universe and the universe was him, where he was
contained by the universe and simultaneously contained it and
everything had an equal dignity, whether animate or inanimate,
an equal value. Rock, tree, horse or man – all were equal. This
was the mystical belief of many of King Mannach's folk. A
visitor from Corum's world might have seen this as primitive
worship of nature, but Corum knew that it was much more
than that. Many a farmer there was in the land of the Tuha-na-
Cremm Croich who would bow politely to a stone and murmur
an apology before moving it from one place to another and
he would treat his earth, his ox and his plough with as much
courtesy as he would treat his father, his wife or his friend.

As a result, life among the Tuha-na-Cremm Croich had a
formal, dignified rhythm which did not rob it of vitality or
humour or, on occasions, anger. And this was why Corum
found pride in fighting the Fhoi Myore, for the Fhoi Myore
threatened more than life. The Fhoi Myore threatened the
quiet dignity of this folk.

Tolerant of their own foibles, their own vanities, their own
follies, the Tuha-na-Cremm Croich tolerated these qualities
in others. It was ironical to Corum that his own race, the
Vadhagh (called Sidhi by this folk now) had at the end been
possessed of a similar outlook and had been robbed of it by
the ancestors of this folk. He wondered if, in achieving such
a noble way of life, a people became automatically vulnerable
to destruction by those who had not achieved it. If so, it was

15

an irony of cosmic proportions. And so Corum dismissed this line of reasoning, for he had become weary of cosmic proportions since his encounter with the Sword Rulers and his discovery of his own destiny.

Now King Fiachadh came a-visiting, risking much to cross the water from the west. His envoy arrived on a steaming horse which was wrenched to a skidding stop at the edge of the great water ditch surrounding the walls of Caer Mahlod. The envoy was clad in billowing pale green silk, silver breastplate and greaves, a silver battle-cap and a surcoat quartered in yellow, blue, white and purple. He panted as he called his business to the guards upon the gate-towers. Corum, running from the other side of the battlements, saw him and was astonished, for he was dressed in a style unlike anything he had seen before in this land.

'King Fiachadh's man!' called the envoy. 'Coming to announce our king's arrival on your shores.' He pointed to the west. 'Our ships have landed. King Fiachadh begs the hospitality of his brother, King Mannach!'

'Wait,' cried a guard. 'We shall tell King Mannach!'

'Then hurry, I beg of you, for we are anxious to seek the security of your walls. We have heard many tales of late concerning the dangers to be found abroad in your land.'

While Corum remained in the gate-tower, looking with polite curiosity at the envoy, King Mannach was summoned.

King Mannach was astonished for other reasons. 'Fiachadh? Why comes he to Caer Mahlod?' he murmured, calling out to the envoy: 'King Fiachadh knows that he is ever welcome in our town. But why journey you from the land of the Tuha-na-Manannan? Are you attacked?'

The envoy was still panting, at first managing only to shake his head.

'Nay, sire. My master wishes to confer with you and only recently we learned that Caer Mahlod had been freed of the Fhoi Myore frost. Thus we set sail speedily, without the usual formalities. For this King Fiachadh wishes you to forgive him.'

'There is nothing to forgive, unless it be the quality of our hospitality, tell King Fiachadh. We await him with pleasant anticipation.'

Another nod and the silk-clad knight forced his horse round to ride towards the cliffs, his loose jerkin and surcoat flapping, his silver cap and horse furniture flashing as he disappeared into the distance.

King Mannach laughed. 'Prince Corum, you will like my old friend Fiachadh. And at last we shall have news of how the folk of the Western Kingdoms fare. I had feared them conquered.'

'I had feared them conquered,' King Mannach said again as he spread his arms.

And the great gates of Caer Mahlod were opened and through the passage (which now led under the moat) came a great parade of knights, maidens and squires, bearing banner-decked lances, with samite cloaks, with buckles and brooches of finely worked red gold set with amethysts, turquoises and mother-of-pearl; with round shields engraved and enamelled in complicated, flowing designs, with silver-bound scabbards and gilded shoes. Tall, handsome women sat astride horses with ribbons plaited in their manes and tails. The men, too, were tall, and had long, thick moustaches of fiery red or warm yellow, their hair either flowing freely below their shoulders or bound in plaits or secured in bunches with little clasps of gold, brass or gem-set iron.

At the centre of this colourful party was a barrel-chested giant of a man with a bright red beard and piercing blue eyes and wind-browned cheeks, dressed in a long robe of red silk trimmed with the fur of the winter fox, and wearing no helmet, only an ancient iron circlet in which runes had been set in delicate, curling gold.

King Mannach's arms were still spread as he spoke joyfully:

'Welcome, old friend. Welcome, King Fiachadh of the Distant West, of the old, green land of our forefathers!'

And the great giant with the red beard opened his mouth and he bellowed with laughter, swinging one leg free over the saddle and sliding to the ground.

'I come in my usual style, you see, Mannach. In all my pomp, in all my bombastic majesty!'

'I see,' said King Mannach embaracing the giant, 'and I am glad. Who would want a Fiachadh otherwise? You bring colour and enchantment to Caer Mahlod. See – my people smile with pleasure. See – their spirits rise. We shall feast tonight. We shall celebrate. You have brought joy to us, King Fiachadh!'

17

King Fiachadh laughed again, with pleasure at King Mannach's words, before turning to regard Corum who had stood back while the old friends greeted one another.

'And this is your Sidhi hero – your name hero – Cremm Croich!'

He stalked towards Corum and placed a huge hand upon Corum's shoulder, looking deeply into Corum's face and appearing to be satisfied. 'I thank you, Sidhi, for what you did to help my brother king. I bring magic with me and we shall talk together later of that. I bring a weighty matter, also . . . ' he turned to King Mannach, 'and that we must all discuss.'

'Is that why you visit us, sire?' Medhbh stepped forward. She had been visiting a friend in a valley some way distant and had arrived just before King Fiachadh. She was still in riding costume, in leather and white linen, her unbound red hair flowing down her back.

'It is the main reason, lovely Medhbh,' said King Fiachadh bending to kiss the cheek she offered. 'You are grown as beautiful as I predicted! Ah, my sister lives again in you.'

'In all ways,' said King Mannach, and there appeared to be a significance in his words which Corum failed to identify.

Medhbh laughed. 'Your compliments are as huge as your vanity, Uncle!'

'But they are as sincere,' said Fiachadh. And he winked.

2. THE TREASURE
BROUGHT BY
KING FIACHADH

King Fiachadh had brought a harpist with
him and for an instant Corum felt a shiver run through him, the
harpist's music was so unearthly. Corum thought he heard the
harp which had sounded at Castle Owyn, but it was not that
harp. This was sweeter. The bard's voice merged with the harp
so that at times it was hard to tell which one heard. Corum
sat with all the others in the great hall of Caer Mahlod, at a
single vast table. Hounds ranged among the benches, nosing
through reeds strewn upon the flagstones for scraps, for pools
of sweet mead. Brands flared brightly, merrily, as if the laughter
on all sides actually brightened the hall. Taking after their
masters, King Fiachadh's knights and ladies sported with the
men and women of Caer Mahlod and many songs were sung,
many boasts shouted, many improbable tales told.

Corum sat between King Mannach and King Fiachadh and
Medhbh sat next to her uncle, all at the head of the great
dining board. King Fiachadh ate as lustily as he spoke, though
Corum noticed that the king took little mead and was by no
means as drunk as his retainers. Neither did King Mannach
drink overmuch, and Corum and Medhbh followed his example. If King Fiachadh chose not to get drunk, there must be
a particularly good reason, for evidently he liked to drink. He
told several tall stories concerning his capacity while they ate.

The feasting went well, and slowly the hall emptied as,

usually in couples, the guests and residents of Caer Mahlod bowed good night and left, and soon there were only a few snoring squires sprawled along the table, a big knight of the Tuha-na-Manannan spreadeagled under the table, a warrior and a maiden of the Tuha-na-Cremm Croich sprawled in each other's arms near the wall.

And King Fiachadh said in a deep, serious voice:

'You are the last I have visited, old friend.' He looked hard at King Mannach. 'I knew already what you would say. I fear I knew, too, what the others would say.'

'Say?' King Mannach frowned.

'To my proposal.'

'You have been visiting other kings?' said Corum. 'All the other kings whose folk are still free?'

King Fiachadh nodded his great, red head. 'All. I see that it is imperative we unite. Our only defence against the Fhoi Myore can be our unity. First I went to the land south of my own – to the folk called Tuha-na-Anu. Secondly I sailed north where dwell, among others, the Tuha-na-Tir-nam-Beo. A mountain people and fierce. Thirdly I sailed down the coast and guested with King Daffynn of the Tuha-na-Gwyddneu Garanhir. Fourthly I came to the Tuha-na-Cremm Croich. Three kings are cautious, thinking that to attract the attention of the Fhoi Myore will mean instant destruction to their lands. What does the fourth king say?'

'What does King Fiachadh ask?' said Medhbh reasonably.

'That all those who remain – four great peoples as far as I know – unite. We have some treasures which the power of the Sidhi could put to use in our favour. We have great warriors. We have your example of defeating them. We should carry the attack to Craig Dôn or Caer Llud, wherever the six remaining Fhoi Myore dwell. A large army. The remains of the free Mabden. What say you, King?'

'I say that I would agree,' said Mannach. 'Who would not?'

'Three kings would not. Each king thinks himself safer by staying in his own land and saying nothing, doing nothing. And all three kings are afraid. They say that with Amergin in the hands of the Fhoi Myore there is no point in fighting. The elected High King is not dead, so a new one cannot be made. The Fhoi Myore knew this when they spared Amergin's life . . .'

'It is not like your folk to let superstition bind them,' said Corum softly. 'Why do you not change this law and make a new High King?'

'It is not superstition,' said King Mannach without offence. 'For one thing, all the kings must meet to elect the new High King and I gather some are afraid to leave their own domain lest those lands be attacked in their absence or lest they are attacked while in other lands. An election of a High King takes many months. All the people must be consulted. All must hear the candidates, speak with them if they wish. Can we break such a law? If we do break our ancient laws, are our customs worth fighting for?'

Medhbh said:

'Make Corum your War Leader. Unify the kingdoms under him.'

'That suggestion had been made,' said King Fiachadh. 'I made it. None would hear of it. Most of us have no reason to trust gods. Gods have betrayed us in the past. We prefer to have no part of them.'

'I am not a god.' said Corum, reasonably.

'You are modest,' said King Fiachadh, 'but you are a god. A demigod at very least.' He stroked his red beard. 'That is what I think. And I have met you. Imagine, then, what those kings who do not know you think. They have heard the tales by now and those tales must have been greatly magnified by the time they reached them. For instance, I thought to meet a being at least twelve feet high!' King Fiachadh smiled, for he was taller than Corum. 'No, the only thing which would unite our folk would be the release of Amergin and the restoration of his full senses.'

'What has become of Amergin?' Corum asked. He had never heard the details of the High King's fate, for the Tuha-na-Cremm Croich were reluctant to discuss them.

'He is under a glamour,' said King Fiachadh soberly.

'An enchantment? What is its nature?'

'We are not sure,' said King Mannach. He continued reluctantly:

'Amergin is said to think of himself now as an animal. Some say he believes he is a goat, others a sheep, others a pig . . . '

'You see how clever are those who serve the Fhoi Myore?' Medhbh said. 'They keep our Archdruid alive but destroy his dignity.'

'And a gloom settles over all those who remain free,' King Fiachadh put in. 'That has much to do with why our fellow kings will not fight, Mannach. They have no soul for it, with Amergin crawling on all fours and eating grass.'

21

'Do not continue,' said King Mannach raising his hand. His old, strong face showed much grief. 'Our own High King symbolizes all our pride . . . '

'Do not confuse the symbol with the reality, however,' said Corum. 'Much pride remains amongst the Mabden race.'

'Aye,' said Medhbh. 'It is true.'

'Nonetheless,' said King Fiachadh, 'our people will only unite under an Amergin free from enchantment. Amergin was so wise. Such a great man was Amergin.' And a tear came to his blue eye. He turned his head away from them.

'Then Amergin must be rescued,' said Corum flatly. 'Should I find your king for you and bring him to the West?' He did not speak impetuously. From the beginning he had considered this. 'Disguised, I might reach Caer Llud.'

And when Fiachadh looked back he was not crying.

He was grinning.

'And I have the disguise,' he said.

Corum laughed aloud. He had been considering a decision, plainly, which King Fiachadh had also been considering – perhaps for much longer.

'You are a Sidhi . . . ' began the king of the Tuha-na-Manannan.

'Related to them,' said Corum, 'as I discovered upon my last quest. We have looks in common and, I suppose, certain powers. I fail to understand, though, why I should possess such powers . . . '

'Because all believe,' said Medhbh simply, and she leaned towards him and touched his arm. The touch was like a kiss. He smiley tenderly at her. 'Very well,' he said. 'Because all believe. However, you may call me "Sidhi" if it suits you, King Fiachadh.'

'Then, Sir Sidhi, know this. In the land of the Distant West, the land of my folk, the Tuha-na-Manannan, came a year since a visitor. His name was Onragh . . . '

'Onragh of Caer Llud!' gasped King Mannach. 'In whose keeping . . . '

'Were the Treasures of Llud, the Sidhi gifts? Aye, And Onragh lost them all from his chariot as he fled the Fhoi Myore and their vassals. Because the Hounds of Kerenos followed, he could not go back. So he lost them – all save one. And that Treasure he brought across the water to the Distant West, to the land of gentle mists and rain. And Onragh of Caer Llud was dying from his wounds which were of great

22

variety. Half of one hand had been gnawed by the Hounds. An ear had been severed by a Ghoolegh flencher. Several knives had found his offal. Dying, he presented into my safekeeping the only Treasure he had saved, though it had not saved him. He could not use it. Only a Sidhi can use it, though I do not understand why, save that it was originally a Sidhi gift, like most of Caer Llud's Treasures, and must have worked for us once. And Onragh, doomed to die believing that he had failed our race, brought news of Amergin the High King. At that time Amergin was still in the great tower which stands by the river close to the centre of Caer Llud. This tower has always been the home of the High King. But Amergin was already under the glamour which makes him believe himself a beast. And he was guarded by many Fhoi Myore vassals – some of whom came with the Fhoi Myore from their own Realm and others, the half-dead like the Ghoolegh, drawn from slain or captured Mabden. But guarded right well, my friends, if Onragh is to be believed. And not all the guards have human shape, I heard. But that is where, doubtless, Amergin is.'

'I will need an excellent disguise,' mused Corum, who privately felt he was doomed to fail in his quest, but who also felt that he must attempt it if only to show his respect for these people.

'I hope I can suggest one,' said King Fiachadh and his massive bulk began to rise as he stood up. 'Is my chest where I asked it to be put, brother?'

King Mannach also rose, smoothing back his white hair. Corum remembered that not long since his hair had also had red in it. But that was before the Fhoi Myore had come. And King Mannach's beard was almost white now, too. Still he was a handsome man, standing almost as tall as broad-shouldered Fiachadh, the gold dollar of his kingship around his firm throat. King Mannach pointed to a corner behind their seats.

'There,' he said. 'There is the chest.'

And King Fiachadh went to the corner and picked up the heavy chest by its golden handles and he carried the chest to the table and, with a grunt, put it down. Then from a pouch at his waist he took some keys and unlocked five strong locks. Then he paused, his piercing blue eyes staring at Corum. And he said something mysterious. He said:

'You are not a traitor, Corum, now.'

'I am not,' said Corum. 'Not now.'

23

'I trust a reformed traitor more than I trust myself,' said King Fiachadh, grinning cheerfully as he opened the lid.

But he opened the chest in such a way that Corum could not see the contents.

King Fiachadh reached into the chest and carefully began to draw something out.

'There,' he said. 'The last of the Treasures of Caer Llud.'

And Corum wondered if the king of the Tuha-na-Manannan were joking, still, for King Fiachadh was displaying in both hands a rather tattered robe; a robe such as the poorest of peasants might be too fastidious to wear. A robe which was patched, torn, faded so that it was impossible to tell the original colour.

Holding it almost gingerly and yet tenderly, as if in awe of the old robe, King Fiachadh offered it to Corum.

'This is your disguise,' said King Fiachadh.

3. CORUM ACCEPTS A GIFT

'Did some hero wear it once?' Corum asked. It was the only explanation for the reverence with which King Fiachadh handled the tattered robe.

'Aye, a hero has worn it, according to our legends, during the first fights with Fhoi Myore.' King Fiachadh seemed puzzled by Corum's question. 'It is often called just The Mantle, but sometimes it is called Arianrod's Cloak – so that strictly speaking it is a heroine's mantle, for Arianrod was a female Sidhi, of great fame and much loved by the Mabden.'

'And so you treasure it,' said Corum. 'And well you might . . .'

Medhbh was laughing, for she knew what he thought.

'You come close to condescending to us, Sir Silverhand,' she said. 'Do you think King Fiachadh a fool?'

'Far from it, but . . .'

'If you knew our legends you would understand the power of that much-worn mantle. Arianrod used it for many great feats before she, herself, was slain by some Fhoi Myore during the last great battle between the Sidhi and the Cold Folk. Some say she slew a whole army of Fhoi Myore single-handed while wearing that cloak.'

'It makes the wearer invulnerable?'

'Not exactly,' said King Fiachadh, still proffering the mantle to Corum. 'Will you accept it, Prince Corum?'

'Gladly I will accept a gift from your hand, King Fiachadh,'
said Corum, remembering his manners, and he reached out and
took the cloak gently, in his fleshly hand and his hand of gleaming silver.

And both hands vanished at the wrists so that it seemed he
was again crippled, though this time worse. Yet he could feel
his fleshly hand and feel the texture of the cloth with his fingers,
for all that the mantle had gone.

'It does work, then,' said King Fiachadh in tones of great
satisfaction. 'I am glad you accepted it with hesitation, Sir
Sidhi.'

Corum began to understand. He drew his fleshly hand away
from under the cloak and there was his hand again!

'A mantle of invisibility?'

'Aye,' said Medhbh in awe. 'The same mantle used by
Gyfech to enter the bedchamber of Bén while her father slept
across the door. That mantle was much prized, even amongst
the Sidhi.'

Corum said: 'I believe I know how it must work. It comes
from another plane. Just as Hy-Breasail is part of another
world, so is this mantle. It shifts the wearer into another plane,
just as the Vadhagh could once move from plane to plane and
remain aware of activities on different planes . . . '

They knew not of what he spoke, but they were too delighted
to question him.

He laughed. 'Brought from the Sidhi plane, it has no true
existence here. Yet why will it not work for Mabden?'

'It will not always work for Sidhi,' said King Fiachadh.
'There are some – Mabden or others – possessed of a sixth sense
which makes them aware of you even when you are invisible to
all others. Very few possess this sixth sense so that you may
wear the mantle without detection most of the time. However,
someone whose sixth sense is well-developed will see you just
as I see you now.'

'And this is the disguise I must use to go to the Towers of
the High King?' Corum said, handling the cloak with care and
equally as much reverence as had King Fiachadh, marvelling as
its folds hid first one portion and then another of his anatomy.
'Yes, it is a good disguise.' He smiled. 'There is none better.' He
handed the mantle back to the king. 'Best keep it safely in its
chest until it is needed.'

And when the chest was locked with all five keys, Corum

sank back in his chair, his expression thoughtful. 'Now,' he said, 'there is much to be planned.'

So it was late before Corum and Medhbh lay together in their wide, low bed, looking out through the windows at the summer moon.

'It was prophesied,' said Medhbh sleepily, 'that Cremm Croich should go upon three quests, face three great dangers, make three strong friendships . . .'

'Prophesied where?'

'In the old legends.'

'You have not mentioned this before.'

'There seemed no point. Legends are vague. You are not what the legends led us to expect, after all.' She smiled quietly.

He returned her smile. 'Well, then, I begin the second quest tomorrow.'

'And you will be gone long from my side,' said Medhbh.

'That is my fate, I fear. I came for duty, not for love, sweet Medhbh. The love must be enjoyed while it does not interfere with duty.'

'You could be killed, could you not? For all you are an elven lord?'

'Aye, killed by sword, or poison. I could even fall from my horse and break my neck!'

'Do not mock my fears, Corum.'

'I am sorry.' He rose on one elbow and looked into her lovely eyes. He bent and kissed her lips. 'I am sorry, Medhbh.'

He rode a red horse, such as he had ridden when he first came to Cremmsmound. Its coat shone in the early morning sunshine. From beyond the walls of Caer Mahlod came the sound of birdsong.

He wore all his ceremonial fighting gear, the ancient gear of the Vadhagh. He wore a shirt of blue samite and his breeks were doeskin. He wore a peaked, conical silver helm with his runic name set into it (the runes were indecipherable to the Mabden) and he wore his byrnie, a layer of silver upon a layer of brass. He wore all save his scarlet robe, his Name-robe, for that he had traded to the wizard Calatin at the place he knew as Moidel's Mount. Upon the horse was a mantle of yellow velvet and harness and saddle were of crimson leather with designs picked out in white.

For weapons Corum took a lance, an axe, a sword and a dirk. The lance was tall, its shaft strengthened with gleaming brass, its head of polished iron. The axe was double-headed, plain and long-hafted, also bound with bands of brass. The sword hung in a scabbard matching the horse's harness and its hilt was dressed in leather, bound with fine gold and silver wire, with a heavy round pommel of bronze. The dirk had been made by the same craftsman and matched the sword.

'Who could mistake you for anything but a demigod?' said King Fiachadh approvingly.

Prince Corum made a small smile and clutched his reins in his silver hand. He reached with his other hand to adjust the plain war-board which hung behind his saddle over one of the panniers containing as well as his provisions a tightly rolled fur cape which he would need as he advanced into Fhoi Myore lands. The other cape, the Sidhi cloak, Arianrod's Cloak, he had rolled and wrapped about his waist. Tucked into this were the gauntlets he would wear later, to protect one hand from the cold and to disguise the other so that he would not be easily recognized by any enemy.

Medhbh tossed back her long red hair and came forward to kiss his fleshly hand, looking up at him with eyes that were both proud and troubled.

'Have care with your life, Corum,' she murmured. 'Preserve it if you can, for all of us will need you even when this quest is over.'

'I shall not throw my life away,' he promised. 'Life has become good for me, Medhbh. But neither do I fear death at this moment.'

He wiped the sweat from his forehead. All his gear made him hot beneath the sun which was already blazing down, but he knew he would not be hot for long. He adjusted the embroidered eye-patch over the blind socket. He touched her gently upon her brown arm. 'I shall come back to you,' he promised.

King Mannach folded his arms across his chest and cleared his throat. 'Bring Amergin to us, Prince Corum. Bring our High King with you.'

'Only if Amergin is with me will I come back to Caer Mahlod. And if I cannot bring him, then I will make every effort to send him to you, King Mannach.'

'This is a great quest, this quest,' said King Mannach. 'Farewell, Corum.'

'Farewell, Corum,' said Fiachadh the red-bearded, putting a large, strong hand upon the Vadhagh's knee. 'Good luck in this.'

'Farewell, Corum,' said Medhbh, and her voice was now as steady as her gaze.

Then Corum kicked at the flanks of his red horse and he went from them.

It was with a calm mind that Corum rode from Caer Mahlod, across the gentle hills, into the deep, cool forest, going east to Caer Llud, listening to the birds, the rush of the little shining streams over old rocks, the whisper of the oaks and the elms.

Not once did Corum look back, not once did he feel a pang of regret, not once did he grieve or know fear or reluctance concerning his quest, for he knew that he fulfilled his destiny and that he represented a great ideal and he was, at that moment, content.

Such contentment was rare, thought Corum, for one destined to take part in the eternal struggle. Perhaps because he did not fight against his destiny this time, because he accepted his duty, he was rewarded with this peculiar peace of mind. He began to wonder if he would find peace only by accepting his fate. It would be a strange paradox – tranquillity attained in strife.

By the evening the sky had begun to grow grey, and heavy clouds could be seen in the horizon towards the east.

4. A WORLD FULL
OF DEATH

Shivering, Corum pulled the heavy fur cloak around his shoulders and drew the hood over his helmeted head. Then he drove his fleshly hand deep into the fur-lined gauntlet he held ready, then he covered his silver hand with the other gauntlet. He stamped out the remains of his fire and looked this way and that across the landscape, his breath billowing white in the air. The sky was a hard, flat blue and it was sunless, for it was not yet true dawn. The land was almost featureless and the ground was dead, black, with a coating of pale frost. Here and there a stark, leafless tree stood out. In the distance was a line of snow-topped hills, as black as the ground. Corum sniffed the wind.

It was a dead wind.

The only scent on the wind was the scent of the killing frost. This part of the land was so desolate that it was evident the Cold Folk had spent some time here. Perhaps this was where they had camped before moving against Caer Mahlod in their war with that city.

Now Corum heard the sound he had thought he had heard before. This sound had caused him to spring up from his fire and disperse the smoke. The sound of hoofbeats. He looked to the south-east. There was a place where the ground rose and obscured his view. It was from beyond the rise that the hoofbeats were coming.

And now Corum heard another sound.

The faint baying of hounds.

The only hounds he might expect to hear in these parts were the devil hounds of Kerenos.

He ran to his red horse, who was showing signs of nervousness, and mounted himself in his saddle, shaking his lance free from its scabbard and laying it across his pommel. He leaned forward and patted his horse's neck to calm the beast. He turned the horse towards the rise, ready to meet the danger.

A single rider appeared first, just as the sun began to rise behind him. The sun's rays caught the rider's armour and it flashed deep red. There was a naked sword in the rider's hand and the sword also reflected the rays of the sun so that for a second Corum could barely see. Then the armour turned to a fierce, burning blue, and Corum guessed the identity of the horseman.

The baying of those frightful hounds became louder, but still they had not appeared.

Corum urged his horse towards the rise.

Suddenly there was silence.

The voices of the hounds were stilled; the rider sat unmoving on his horse, but his armour changed colour again, from blue to greenish yellow.

Corum listened to the sound of his own breathing, the steady beating of his own horse's hooves upon hard, rimed earth. He began to ascend the rise, approaching the rider, his lance ready.

And then the rider spoke from within the featureless helm enclosing his head.

'Ha! I guessed so. It is you, Corum.'

'Good morning, Gaynor. Will you joust?'

Prince Gaynor the Damned threw back his head and laughed a bleak, hollow laugh and his armour changed from yellow to blazing black and he swept his sword into its scabbard.

'You know me, Corum. I am become wary. I do not have it in mind to make another journey into Limbo just yet. Here, at least, I have matters to occupy my time. There – well, there is nothing at all there.'

'In Limbo.'

'Aye. In Limbo.'

'Join a noble cause, then. Fight for my cause. Thus you could win redemption.'

'Redemption? Oh, Corum, you are simple-minded indeed. Who would redeem me?'

'No one.'

'Then why do you speak of redemption?'

'You can redeem yourself. That is what I meant. I do not mean that you should placate the Lords of Law – if they still exist anywhere – or that you should bow to any authority save your own pride. I mean that there is within you, Prince Gaynor the Damned, something which could save you from the hopelessness now consuming you. You know those whom you serve to be degenerate, destructive, lacking in greatness of spirit. Yet wilfully you follow them, fulfil their ends for them, perpetrate great crimes and create monstrous miseries, spread evil, carry death – you know what you do and you know, too, that for you such crimes bring further agony of spirit.'

The armour changed from black to angry crimson. Prince Gaynor's faceless helm turned to stare directly into the rising sun. His horse stirred and he tightened his grip upon his reins.

'Join my cause, Prince Gaynor. I know that you respect it.'

'Law has rejected me,' said Prince Gaynor the Damned in a hard, weary voice. 'All that I once followed, all that I once respected, all that I once admired and sought to emulate – all have rejected Gaynor. It is too late, you see, Prince Corum.'

'It is not too late,' said Corum urgently, 'and you forget, Gaynor, that I alone have looked upon that face you hide behind your helm. I have seen all your guises, all your dreams, all your secret desires, Gaynor.'

'Aye,' said Prince Gaynor the Damned quietly, 'and that is why you must perish, Corum. That is why I cannot bear to know that you are alive.'

'Then fight,' said Corum with a sigh. 'Fight now.'

'I would not dare do that, not now that you have beaten me in combat once. I would not have you look upon all my faces again, Corum. No, you must die by other means than in single combat. The Hounds . . . '

Then Corum, guessing what was in Gaynor's mind, sent his horse into a sudden gallop, lance aimed directily at Gaynor's featureless helm, and rushed upon his ancient enemy.

But Gaynor laughed and wheeled his steed, thundering down the hill so that the white frost rose in glistening shards on all sides of him and the ground seemed to crack as he crossed it.

And Gaynor rode straight down the hill towards where half a score of pale hounds squatted, their red tongues lolling, their yellow eyes glaring, their yellow fangs dripping yellow saliva, their long, feathery tails curled along their shaggy backs. And all their bodies were a glowing, leprous white, save for the tips of their ears which were the colour of fresh-drawn blood. Some, the largest, were the size of small ponies.

And now they were getting to their feet as Gaynor rode towards them. And now they were panting and grinning as Gaynor yelled to them.

And now they were running up the hill towards Corum.

Corum spurred his horse to greater efforts, hoping to plunge through the dogs and reach Gaynor before he escaped. He struck the pack with an impact which bowled several of the hounds over and his lance skewered one directly through the skull. And both these things combined to slow Corum down as he tried to tug the lance from the dog he had slain. His horse reared, screaming, and lashed at the dogs with its iron-shod hooves.

Corum abandoned his grip upon his lance and swung his double-bladed war-axe from his back, whirling it as he struck first to his left and then to his right, cleaving the head from one dog and cracking the spine of another. But the dogs kept up their chill baying and this mixed with the horrible howling of the hound whose spine had been snapped and yellow fangs clashed on Corum's byrnie and ripped at his great fur cloak and tried to drag the whistling war-axe from his hands. And Corum kicked his right foot free from his stirrup and drove his heel into the snout of one hound while with his axe he smashed down a dog which had got a grip upon his horse's harness. But the horse was tiring fast and Corum realized that it could hold out against the hounds only a few moments more before it collapsed beneath him with its throat torn, and there were still some dogs to contend with.

Five. Corum sliced the rear legs from a dog which sought to spring at him and misjudged its distance. The thing flopped to the ground near the one which still died from a broken spine. The dog with the broken spine dragged itself to where its comrade writhed and sank its fangs into the red, exposed flanks, tearing hungrily at the flesh, taking a final meal before it expired.

Then Corum heard a yell and got an impression of something black moving to the right of him. Gaynor's men, no doubt, coming in to finish him. He tried a back-swipe with the axe, but missed.

The Hounds of Kerenos were regrouping, readying themselves for a more organized attack upon him. Corum knew he could not fight both the hounds and the newcomers, whoever they were. He looked for a gap in the ranks of the dogs through which he might gallop. But his horse stood panting now, its legs trembling, and he knew he could get nothing more from the beast. He transferred his axe to his silver hand and drew his sword. Then he began to jog towards the hounds, preferring to die attacking them rather than fleeing from them.

And again something black swept past him. A fast-moving pony with a rider crouched low upon its back, a curved sword in both hands, slicing into the white backs so that they yelped in surprise and scattered, whereupon Corum selected one and rode after it, bearing it down. It turned, going for his horse's throat, but Corum stabbed and took the creature in the chest. Its long-clawed paws scrabbled at the body of the skittering horse for a moment before it fell to the ground.

And now only three hounds lived. Three hounds running after the black speck of a rider who could still be seen in the distance, his armour changing colour even as he rode.

Then Corum dismounted from his horse and drew a deep breath and then regretted it for the stink of the hounds was worse in death than in life. He looked around him at the ruin of white fur and red vitals, at the gore which soaked the ground, and then he turned to look at the ally who had appeared to save his life.

His ally was still mounted. His ally grinned and sheathed first one curved sword and then another. He adjusted a broad-brimmed hat upon his long hair. He took a bag which hung from his saddle pommel and he opened it. From the bag crept a small black and white cat which was unusual in that it had a pair of wings neatly folded along its back.

Corum's ally grinned even more widely as he noted Corum's astonishment.

'This situation is not new to me, at least,' said Jhary-a-Conel, the self-styled Companion to Heroes. 'I am often in time to save some champion's life. It is my fate, just as it is his fate to struggle forever in the great wars of history: I sought you at Caer Mahlod, having some intimation that I would be useful but you had already gone. I followed as swiftly as I could, sensing that your life was in peril.'

Jhary-a-Conel swept off his wide-brimmed hat and bowed in his saddle. 'Greetings, Prince Corum.'

Corum was still panting from his fight. He could not speak. But he managed to grin back at his old friend.

'Do you quest with me, Jhary?' he said at last. 'Do you come with me to Caer Llud?'

'If the fates so will it. Aye. How fare you, Corum, in this world?'

'Better than I thought. And better still now that you are here, Jhary.'

'You know I might not be enabled to stay here?'

'I understood as much from our last conversation. And you? Have you had adventures on other planes since we last met?'

'One or two. One or two. Where you are called Hawkmoon, I had one of the most peculiar experiences of my everlasting career.'

And Jhary told Corum the story of his adventures with Hawkmoon, who had gained a friend, lost a bride, found himself inhabiting another's body, and had spent what Corum considered a rather confusing time in a world which was not his own.

As Jhary talked, the two old friends rode from the scene of the slaughter, following in the tracks of Prince Gaynor the Damned who appeared to be riding hastily for Caer Llud.

And Caer Llud was still many, many days distant.

5. THE LANDS WHERE THE FHOI MYORE RULE

'Aye,' said Jhary-a-Conel as he slapped gloved hands together over a fire which seemed reluctant to burn. 'The Fhoi Myore are fitting cousins to the Lords of Entropy, for they seem to seek the same ends. For all I know the Fhoi Myore are what those lords have become. There are so many fluctuations, these days. Caused partially, I should say, by Baron Kalan's foolish manipulation of time, partially as a result of the Million Spheres beginning to slide out of conjunction – though that will take a little while before it is fully accomplished. In the meantime we live in times which are uncertain in more ways than one. The fate of sentient life itself sometimes seems to me to be at stake. Yet do I fear? No, I think not. I place no special value upon sentience. I'd as cheerfully become a tree!'

'Who's to say they are not sentient?' Corum smiled as he set a pan upon the fire and began to lay strips of meat in the slowly boiling water.

'Well, then, a block of marble.'

'Again, we do not know . . . ' Corum began, but Jhary cut him short with a snort of impatience.

'I'll not play such children's games!'

'You misunderstand me. You have touched on a subject I have been considering only lately, you see. I, too, am beginning to realize that there is no special value to being, as it were, able

36

to think. Indeed, one can see many disadvantages. The whole condition of mortals is created by their ability to analyze the universe and their inability to understand it.'

'Some do not care,' said Jhary. 'I, for one, am content to drift – to let whatever happens happen without bothering to ask why it happens.'

'Indeed, I agree that that is an admirable feeling. But we are not all endowed with such feelings by nature. Some must culti-vate those feelings. Others may never cultivate them and they lead unhappy lives as a result. Yet does it matter if our lives are happy or unhappy? Should we place more value on joy than on sorrow? Is it not possible to see both as possessing the same value?'

'All I know,' said Jhary practically, 'is that most of us con-sider it better to be happy . . . '

'Yet we all achieve that happiness in a variety of ways. Some by cultivating carelessness, some by caring. Some by service to themselves and some by service to others. Currently I find pleasure in serving others. The whole question of morality . . . '

'Is as nothing when one's stomach rumbles,' said Jhary, peer-ing into the pan. 'Is that meat done, do you think, Corum?'

Corum laughed. 'I think I am becoming a bore,' he said.

'It's nothing.' Jhary fished pieces of meat from the pan and dropped them into his bowl. He set one piece aside to cool for the cat which purred as it sat on his shoulder and rubbed its head against Jhary's. 'You have found a religion, that is all. What else can you expect in a Mabden dream?'

They rode beside a frozen river, along a track now completely hidden by snow, climbing higher and higher into the hills. They rode past a house whose stone walls had been cracked open as if by the blow of a gigantic hammer and it was only when they were close did they see the white skulls peering from the win-dows and the white hands gesturing in attitudes of terror. The bones shimmered in the pale sunshine.

'Frozen,' said Jhary. 'And cold it was which doubtless cracked the stones.'

'Balahr's work,' said Corum. 'He of the single, deadly eye. I know him. I have fought him.'

And they went past the house and over the hill and they found a town where the frozen corpses lay strewn about and these still had flesh on them and had plainly died before the cold had frozen them. And each male had been horribly desecrated.

'The work of Goim,' said Corum. 'The only female of the Fhoi Myore still surviving. She has a taste for certain morsels of mortal flesh.'

'We are at the borders of the lands where the Fhoi Myore hold full sway,' said Jhary-a-Conel, pointing ahead to where grey cloud boiled. 'Shall we suffer so? Shall Balahr or Goim find us?'

'It is possible,' Corum told him.

Jhary grinned. 'You are most sober, old friend. Well, console yourself that if they do these things to us we shall remain in a position of moral superiority.'

Corum grinned back.

'It does console me,' he said.

And they led their horses out of the town and down a steep, snow-filled track, passing a cart full of the frozen bodies of children doubtless sent to flee the place before the Fhoi Myore descended.

And they entered a valley where the bodies of a whole army of warriors had been eaten by dogs and here they found fresh tracks – the tracks of a single rider and three large hounds.

'Gaynor also goes this way,' said Corum, 'a mere few hours ahead of us. Why does he dally now?'

'Perhaps he watches us. Perhaps he tries to guess the purpose of our quest,' Jhary suggested. 'With such information he can return to his masters and be welcomed.'

'If the Fhoi Myore welcome anyone. They do not recruit help, as such. There are some – the resurrected dead among them – who have no choice but to follow them and do their work for them, for they are welcome nowhere else.'

'How do the Fhoi Myore resurrect the dead?'

'There is one of the six called Rhannon, I believe. Rhannon breathes cold breath into the mouths of the dead and brings them to life. He kisses the living and introduces them to death. That is the legend. But few know much of the Fhoi Myore. Even the Fhoi Myore hardly know what they do or why they are upon this plane. Once they were driven away by the Sidhi who came from another plane themselves to help the people of Lwym-an-Esh. But with the decline of the Sidhi, the Fhoi Myore strength grew unchecked until they were able to return to the land and begin their conquerings. Their diseases must kill them soon. Few, I understand, will live for more than another thousand years. Then, when the Fhoi Myore die, the whole of this world shall be dead.'

'It would seem,' said Jhary-a-Conel, 'that we could do with a few Sidhi allies.'

'The only one I know is called Goffanon and he is weary of fighting. He accepts that the world is doomed and that nothing he can do will avert that doom.'

'He could be right,' said Jhary feelingly, looking about him.

And then Corum lifted his head, peering this way and that, his face troubled.

Jhary was surprised. 'What is it?'

'Do you not hear it?' Corum looked up into the hills from which they had come.

He could hear it quite plainly now – melancholy, wild, somehow mocking. The strains of a harp.

'Who would play music here?' Jhary murmured. 'Save a dirge?' He listened again. 'And it sounds as if it could be a dirge.'

'Aye,' said Corum grimly. 'A dirge for me. I have heard the harp more than once since I came to this realm, Jhary. And I have been told to fear a harp.'

'It is beautiful, however,' said Jhary.

'I have been told to fear beauty, also,' said Corum. He still could not find the source of the music. He realized that he was trembling and he controlled himself, urging his horse onward. 'I have been told that I shall be slain,' he continued, 'by a brother.'

And Jhary, asking questions, could get Corum to speak no further on this subject. They rode for some miles in silence until they came out of the valley and looked upon a wide plain.

'The Plain of Craig Dôn,' said Corum. 'It is all it can be. This is thought a holy place by the Mabden. We are more than half-way to Caer Llud now, I think.'

'And well into the Lands of the Fhoi Myore,' added Jhary-a-Conel.

Even as they watched a blizzard swept suddenly over the great plain from east to west and was gone again, leaving fresh snow sparkling as a woman might lay a fresh sheet upon a bed.

'We'll leave good tracks in that,' said Jhary.

Corum was marvelling at the strange sight as the fast-moving blizzard moved away into the distance. Overhead the sun was fully obscured by clouds. The clouds were agitated. They swirled restlessly all the time, changing shape swiftly.

'I am reminded somewhat of the Realm of Chaos,' Jhary told him. 'And I have been told that such frozen landscapes as these are the ultimate landscapes of worlds where the Lords of Entropy are triumphant. This is what their wasteful variety achieves. But I speak of other worlds and other heroes – indeed, of other dreams. Shall we risk the dangers of detection upon that plain, or shall we circle the plain and hope that we are not seen?'

'We cross the Plain of Craig Dôn,' said Corum firmly. 'And if we are stopped and have time to speak, we shall say that we have come to offer our services to the Fhoi Myore, knowing that the Mabden cause is hopeless.'

'There seem few here of any intelligence, as I understand by intelligence,' said Jhary. 'Will they give us that time to converse, do you think?'

'We must hope that there are more like Gaynor.'

'An odd thing to hope!' exclaimed Jhary. He smiled at his cat, but it merely purred without apparently understanding its master's joke.

The wind howled then and Jhary bowed to it, pretending to assume that it was showing its appreciation.

Corum clutched his fur robe to him. Though it had been ripped in several places by the Hounds of Kerenos, it was still serviceable.

'Come,' he said. 'Let us cross the Plain of Craig Dôn.'

The snow was in constant movement beneath their horses' feet, eddying like an agitated river over rocks. The wind blew it this way and that. The wind made the snow-drifts heave and fall and reform. The wind drove into their bones so that sometimes they felt they would rather have cold steel in them than that wind. The wind sighed like a huntsman satisfied by his kill. The wind moaned like a satiated lover. The wind growled like a hungry beast. The wind shouted like a conqueror and it hissed like a striking snake. It blew fresh snow from the sky. Their shoulders would be heaped with this snow until it was blown clear again and a new deposit laid in its place. The wind blew roads through the snow for them and then sealed them up again. The wind blew from the east and from the north and from the west and the south. Sometimes it seemed that the wind blew from all directions at once, seeking to crush them as they pressed on across the Plain of Craig Dôn. The wind built castles and it tore them down. The wind whispered promises and roared threats. The wind toyed with them.

Then, through the swirl and the confusion, Corum saw dark shapes ahead. At first he thought them warriors and drew his sword, dismounting, for his horse would be of no help to him in this depth of snow. He sank to his knees in the stuff. Jhary remained on horseback, however.

'Fear not,' he said to Corum. 'They are not men. They are stones. They are the stones of Craig Dôn.'

And Corum realized that he had misjudged the distance, that the objects were still some good distance ahead.

'This is the holy place of the Mabden,' said Jhary.

'This is where they elect their High Kings and hold their important ceremonies,' said Corum.

'It is where they once did these things,' Jhary corrected him.

The wind appeared to drop as they approached the great stones. Even the wind seemed to show reverence for this great, old place. There were seven circles in all, each circle containing another until the centre was reached and the inner circle contained a large stone altar. Looking out from the centre and down the hill, Corum fancied the stone circles represented ripples upon a pool, planes of reality, representations of a geometry not wholly connected with earthly geometry.

'It is a holy place,' he murmured. 'It is.'

'Certainly it touches upon something I cannot explain,' Jhary agreed. 'Does it not remind you in some ways of Tanelorn?'

'Tanelorn? Perhaps. Is this their Tanelorn?'

'Geographically speaking, I think it might be. Tanelorn is not always a city. Sometimes it is a thing. Sometimes it is merely an idea. And this – this is the representation of an idea.'

'So primitive in its materials and the working of those materials,' said Corum. 'Yet so subtle in its conception. What minds created Craig Dôn, I wonder?'

'Mabden minds. Those you serve. This, too, is why they cannot bring themselves to unite against the Fhoi Myore. This was the centre of their world. It reminded them of their faith and their dignity. Now that they can no longer come upon their two great yearly visits to Craig Dôn their souls starve and, starving, rob them of their strength of will.'

'We must find a means of giving Craig Dôn back to them, then,' said Corum firmly.

'But first give them their High King, he who possesses all the wisdom of those who spend whole weeks fasting and meditating at Craig Dôn's altar.' Jhary leaned against one of the great stone pillars. 'Or so they say,' he added, as if embarrassed by having been caught uttering an approving word for the place. 'Not that it is my affair,' he went on. 'I mean, if . . .'

'Look who comes,' said Corum. 'And he appears to come alone.'

It was Gaynor. He had appeared at the outer circle of stones and seemed so small at that distance that he could only be identified by his armour which, as usual, constantly changed colour. He was not on horseback. He came walking through what was almost a tunnel made up of seven great arches and as he came in earshot he said:

'Some would have it that this temple, this Craig Dôn, is a representation of the Million Spheres, of the various planes of existence. But I do not think the local people sophisticated enough to understand such matters, do you?'

'Sophistication is not always measured by an ability to forge good steel or build large cities, Prince Gaynor,' said Corum.

'Indeed no. I am sure that you are right. I have known worlds where the complexity of the natives' thought was equalled only by the squalor of their living conditions.' The faceless helm turned to look up at the boiling sky. 'More snow coming, I'd say. What do you think?'

'Have you been here long, Prince Gaynor?' said Corum, his hand upon the hilt of his sword.

'On the contrary, you seem to have preceded me. I have just arrived.'

'But you knew we should be here?'

'I guessed this was your destination.'

Corum tried to hide his interest. Gaynor was wrong. This was not his destination. But did Gaynor know a secret concerning Craig Dôn? A secret which might be to the advantage of the Mabden.

'This place seems free of wind,' he said. 'At least, it is freer than the plain itself. And no signs of the Fhoi Myore in Craig Dôn itself.'

'Of course not. That is why you sought its sanctuary. You hope to understand why the Fhoi Myore fear it. You think you can find a means of defeating them here.' Gaynor laughed. 'I knew that was your quest.'

Corum restrained a secret smile. Without realizing it Gaynor had betrayed his masters.

'You are clever, Prince Gaynor.'

Gaynor had come to a stop under an arch in the third circle. He moved no closer.

In the distance Corum heard the baying of the Hounds of Kerenos. He smiled openly now.

'Your dogs fear this place, too?'

'Aye – they are Fhoi Myore dogs, come with them from Limbo. Their instincts warn them against Craig Dôn. Only Sidhi and mortals – even mortals such as I – can come here. And I fear the place, too, though I've little reason for my fears. The vortex cannot swallow Gaynor the Damned.'

Corum restrained his impulse to ask Prince Gaynor further questions. He must not let his old enemy know that he had not, until recently, any hint of Craig Dôn's properties.

'Yet you, too, are from Limbo,' Corum reminded Gaynor. 'I cannot understand why the – the vortex does not claim you.'

'Limbo is not my natural home. I was banished there – banished by you, Corum. Only those who came originally from Limbo need fear Craig Dôn. But what you think to gain from coming here, I know not. As naïve as ever, Corum, you doubtless hoped that the Fhoi Myore knew nothing of Craig Dôn and would follow you here. Well, my friend, I must tell you that my masters, while apparently stupid in some matters, have a proper regard for this place. They would not come an inch within the outer circle. Your journey has been for nothing.'

Gaynor laughed his bleak laugh. 'Only once were your Sidhi ancestors successful in luring their foes to this place. Only once did the Fhoi Myore warriors find themselves engulfed and drawn back to Limbo. And that was many centuries ago. Beastlike, the remaining Fhoi Myore keep a safe distance from Craig Dôn, barely realizing why they do so.'

'They would not rather return to their own Realm?'

'They do not understand that that is where they would go. And it is scarcely in the interest of those, like me, who *do* know, to try to communicate this knowledge to them. I have no wish to be abandoned here without their protecting power!'

'So,' said Corum as if to himself, 'my journey has been fruitless.'

'Aye. Moreover I think it unlikely you'll return to Caer Mahlod alive. When I go back to Caer Llud I shall tell them I have seen their Sidhi foe. Then all the hounds will come. All the hounds, Corum. I suggest you remain here, where you are safe.' Gaynor laughed again. 'Stay in this sanctuary. There is nowhere else in this land that you can escape the Fhoi Myore and the Hounds of Kerenos.'

'But,' replied Corum, pretending to miss Gaynor's meaning, 'we have food only for a while. We should starve here, Gaynor.'

'Possibly,' said Gaynor with evident relish. 'On the other hand I could come from time to time with food – when it pleased me. You could live for years, Corum. You could experience something of what I felt while I enjoyed my banishment in Limbo.'

'So that is what you hope for. That is why you did not harry us on our way here!' Jhary-a-Conel began to descend the hill, drawing one of his curved blades.

'No!' Corum cried out to his friend. 'You cannot harm him, Jhary, but he can slay you!'

'It will be pleasant,' Gaynor said, retreating slowly as Jhary came to a reluctant stop. 'It will be pleasant to see you squabbling for the scraps I bring. It will be pleasant to see your friendship die as hunger grows. Perhaps I'll bring you a hound's corpse – one that you slew, Jhary-a-Conel, eh? Would that be tasty? Or perhaps you will begin to find human flesh wholesome. Which one of you will first begin to desire to slay and eat the other?'

'This is an ignoble vengeance that you take, Gaynor,' said Corum.

'It was an ignoble fate you sent me to, Corum. Besides, I do not claim nobility of spirit. That is your province, is it not?'

Gaynor turned and his step was almost light as he walked away from them.

'I will leave the dogs,' he said. 'I am sure you'll appreciate their company.'

Corum watched Gaynor until he had reached the outer circle and climbed on to his horse. The wind made a low sound in the distance, a melancholy murmuring, as if it wished to enter the seven stone rings but could not.

'So,' said Corum musingly, 'we have gained something from the encounter. Craig Dôn is more than a holy place. It is a place of great power – an opening between the Fifteen Realms, perhaps – or even more. We were right to be reminded of Tanelorn, Jhary-a-Conel. But how is the gateway formed? What ritual opens it? Perhaps the High King will know.'

'Aye,' said Jhary, 'we have, as you say, gained something,

Corum. But we have lost something, too. How are we to reach the High King now? Listen.'

And Corum listened, and he heard the ferocious baying of the frightful Hounds of Kerenos as they ranged about the outer stone circle. If they rode from the sanctuary of Craig Dôn, the dogs would instantly be upon them.

Corum frowned and he shivered as he drew his fur cloak about him. He squatted by the altar while Jhary-a-Conel paced back and forth and the horses snorted nervously as they pricked their ears and heard the hounds. It seemed to become colder as the evening settled upon the place of the seven stone circles. Craig Dôn's properties might protect them from the Fhoi Myore, but they could not protect them from the marrow-chilling cold, neither were there materials here from which they could build a fire.

Night came down. The noise of the wind increased, but it could not drown the persistent and terrible howling of the Hounds of Kerenos.

Book Two

In which Price Corum makes
use of one Treasure only to
discover his lack of two others . . .

1. A SAD CITY
IN THE MIST

They stood between two of the great stone pillars of Craig Dôn and faced the prowling devil dogs of the Fhoi Myore. The Hounds of Kerenos were both fierce and wary; they snapped, they snarled, but they gave the stone circle wide clearance. Others of the dogs sat some distance off, barely visible against the wind-swirled snow which ruffled their shaggy coats. From somewhere Gaynor had added five more hounds.

Corum narrowed his eyes and fixed them on the nearest dog, then he drew back the arm which held the long and heavy lance, shifted his feet a little to get the best balance, and hurled the weapon with all the force of his fear, his anger and his desperation.

The lance flew true, driving deep into the canine body, knocking the hound from its feet.

'Now!' called Corum; and Jhary-a-Conel, who held the end of the rope, began to tug. Corum pulled too.

The line had been securely attached to the lance and the lance was buried deep in the dog's body so that this, too, was dragged back into the sanctuary of the stone circle. The hound still lived and when it realized what was happening to it it began to make feeble efforts to get free. It whined, it tried to snap at the shaft of the lance, but then it had been pulled under the arch and it became suddenly supine as if it accepted its doom. It died.

Corum and Jhary-a-Conel were jubilant. Putting his booted foot on the carcass Corum jerked his lance free and immediately ran back to the arch, selecting a fresh target, hurling his weapon out with the line flicking behind it, striking a second hound in the throat and instantly dragging the lance back. This time the lance came free from the corpse and bounced back through the snow to them. Now there were six beasts left. But they had become more wary. Not for the first time, Corum wished that he had brought his bone bow and his arrows upon this quest.

A hound came forward and sniffed at the corpse of its fellow. It nuzzled the throat from where the fresh blood poured. It began to lap the blood with its long, red tongue.

And a third hound paid dearly for its meal as the lance sprang out again from between the tall columns and plunged into its left flank. The hound yelled, whirled, tried to get free, fell writhing into the blood-flecked snow, rose again and wrenched itself away, leaving a large part of its flank in the head of the spear. It ran in circles for a while as its life-blood gushed from it and then, about a hundred yards from the corpse it had only recently been feeding from, it flopped down.

Feeling that they were at a safe distance from the deadly lance, its brother hounds moved in and began to feast off its still living flesh.

'It is our one great advantage,' said Corum as he and Jhary-a-Conel mounted their horses, 'that the Hounds of Kerenos possess no moral sense concerning the eating of their fellows! It is their weakness, I think.'

Then, while the hounds slavered around their feast, Corum and Jhary-a-Conel rode back through the seven circles, past the carved stone altar at the centre of the first circle, out again through the circles until they were on the far side from the hounds.

The hounds had not yet guessed Corum's plan. There were a few minutes in hand.

Digging their heels deep into the flanks of their horses, they galloped as fast as they could away from Craig Dôn, heading not for Caer Mahlod (as Gaynor would think they did) but for their original destination of Caer Llud. With any luck the wind would obscure their tracks and spread their scent in all directions and they would have time to reach Caer Llud and find Amergin the Archdruid before Gaynor or the Fhoi Myore had any hint of their plan.

Gaynor had spoken the truth when he had told them that they could never reach Caer Mahlod with all the Hounds of Kerenos hunting for them, but when Gaynor found them gone it was almost certain that for a while he would waste time riding in the wrong direction while his dogs cast for their scent. But Gaynor's jaundiced view of mortal character had worked this time to his disadvantage. He had reckoned without the quick thinking of Corum and Jhary-a-Conel, without their determination or their willingness to risk their lives for a cause. He had spent too long in the company of the weak, the greedy and the decadent. Doubtless he preferred such company, since he shone in it.

As he rode, Corum considered what he had learned from Gaynor the Damned. Did Craig Dôn still possess the properties Gaynor had described or had they only worked for the Sidhi? Was Craig Dôn now only a shell, avoided by the Fhoi Myore out of superstition rather than knowing respect for its powers? He hoped that there would come a time when he could discover the truth for himself. If Craig Dôn was still truly a place of power there might be a way found to make use of it again.

But now he must forget Craig Dôn as the pillars grew to black shadows in the distance and then were obscured entirely by the swirling snow. Now he must think ahead, of Caer Llud and Amergin under a glamour in his tower by the river, guarded both by men and things which were not men.

They were cold and they were hungry. The coats of their horses were rimed and their own cloaks sparkled with frost. Their faces were numbed by the cold wind and their bodies ached whenever they moved.

But they had found Caer Llud. They drew rein upon a hill and saw a wide, frozen river. On both banks of the river and connected by well-constructed wooden bridges was the City of the High King, pale granite coated with snow, some of the buildings rising several storeys. For this world it was a large city, perhaps the largest, and must once have contained a population of twenty or thirty thousand.

But now the city had the appearance of having been

abandoned, for all that shapes could be seen moving through the mist which hung in its streets.

The mist was everywhere. Thinner in some places, it clung to Caer Llud like a threadbare shroud. Corum recognized the mist. It was Fhoi Myore mist. It was the mist which followed the Cold Folk wherever they travelled in their huge, poorly made wicker war-carts. Corum feared that mist, as he feared the primitive, amoral power of the surviving Lords of Limbo. Even as they watched, he saw a movement where the mist was thickest, close to the river bank. He saw a suggestion of a dark, horned head, of a gigantic torso which faintly resembled the body of a toad, of the outlines of a huge, creaking cart drawn by something as oddly formed as the rider. Then it had gone.

From Corum's frost-cracked lips came a single word:

'Kerenos.'

'He who is master to the Hounds?' Jhary sniffed.

'And master of much more.' Corum added.

Jhary blew his nose upon a large linen rag he took from under his jerkin. 'I fear this weather affects my health badly,' he said. 'I would not mind coming to blows with some of those who created such weather!'

Corum shook his head. 'We are not strong enough, you and I. We must wait. We must be as careful to avoid conflict with the Fhoi Myore as Gaynor is in avoiding direct conflict with me.' He peered through the mist and the eddying snow. 'Caer Llud is not guarded. Plainly they fear no attack from the Mabden. Why should they? That is to our advantage.'

He looked at Jhary's face which was blue with cold. 'I think we'd both pass for living corpses if we entered Caer Llud now. If stopped, we shall announce that we are Fhoi Myore men. While it is imposible to reason either with the Fhoi Myore or their slaves, because of their primitive mentalities, it also means that they are slow to recognize a deception. Come.' Corum urged his horse down the hill towards that sad city, that once great city of Caer Llud.

Leaving the relatively clean air for the mist of Caer Llud was like going from midsummer into midwinter. If Corum and Jhary-a-Conel had considered themselves cold, it was now as nothing to the totality of coldness in which they now found themselves. The mist seemed virtually sentient, eating into their flesh, their bones and their vitals so that they were hard-put not to cry out and reveal their ordinary humanity.

For Gaynor the Damned, for the Ghoolegh, the living dead, for the Brothers of the Pines, like Hew Argech whom Corum had once fought, such cold doubtless meant little. But for mortals of the conventional mould it meant a great deal. Corum, gasping, shuddering, wondered if they could hope to live through it. With set faces they rode on, avoiding the worst of the mist as best they could, seeking the great tower by the river where they hoped Amergin was still imprisoned.

They said nothing as they rode, fearing to reveal their identities, for it was impossible to know who or what lurked on either side of them in the mist. The movement of their horses became sluggish, plodding, as the dreadful mist affected them. At last Corum bent over and spoke close to Jhary's head, finding speech painful as he said:

'There is a house just to the left of us which seems empty. See. The door is open. Ride directly through.'

And he turned his own horse into the doorway and entered a narrow passage already occupied by an old woman and a girl child who were huddled together, frozen and dead. He dismounted and led his horse into a room off the passage.

The room appeared untouched by looters. Mould grew on food on the table which had been set for some ten people. A few spears stood in a corner and there were shields and swords against the wall. The men of the house had gone to fight the Fhoi Myore and had not returned for the meal. The old woman and the girl had died beneath the influence of Balahr's frightful eye. Doubtless they would find the corpses of others – old or young – who had not joined the hopeless battle against the Fhoi Myore when they had first come to Caer Llud. Corum desperately wished to light a fire, to warm his aching bones, to drive the mist from his body, but he knew that this would be risking too much. The living dead did not need fires to warm them and neither did the People of the Pines.

As Jhary-a-Conel led his own horse into the room, drawing a shuddering winged black and white cat from within his jerkin, Corum whispered: 'There will be clothing upstairs, perhaps blankets. I will see.' The small black and white cat was already climbing back inside Jhary's jacket, mewling a complaint.

Corum cautiously climbed a wooden staircase and found himself on a narrow landing. As he had guessed there were others here – two very old men and three babies. The old men had died trying to give their body-heat to the children.

Corum entered a room and found a large cupboard full of blankets stiff with cold. But they were not frozen through. He dragged out as many as he could carry and took them back down the stairs. Jhary seized them gratefully and began to drape them around his shoulders.

Corum was unwrapping something from his waist. It was the nondescript mantle, the gift of King Fiachadh, the Sidhi cloak.

Their plan was already made. Jhary-a-Conel would wait here with the horses while Corum sought Amergin. Corum unfolded the mantle, wondering again as it hid his hands from his own sight. This was the first Jhary had seen of the cloak and he gasped as, huddling in a mound of blankets, he saw what it did.

Then Corum paused.

From the street outside there came sounds. Cautiously he went to the shuttered windows and peered through a crack. Through the clinging mist he saw shapes moving – many shapes. Some were on foot and some were mounted, but all were of the same greenish hue. And Corum recognized them – the strange Brothers to the Pines who had once been men but now had sap instead of blood in their veins and they drew their vitality not from meat and drink but from the earth itself. These were the Fhoi Myore's fiercest fighters, their most intelligent slaves. And the horses they rode were also of the same, strange green colour, kept alive by the same elements which kept the People of the Pines alive. And yet even these were doomed, thought Corum as he watched, when the Fhoi Myore poisoned all the earth so that even the hardy trees could no longer live. But by that time the Fhoi Myore would no longer need their green warriors.

These were the creatures of whom Corum was most wary, with the exception of Gaynor himself, for they still retained much of their former intellect. He motioned Jhary to complete silence and barely breathed as he watched the throng pass by.

It was a large army and it had prepared itself for an expedition. It was leaving Caer Llud it seemed. Was it to make a further attack on Caer Mahlod, or did they march elsewhere?

And then, behind this army, swam a thicker mist and from out of the mist came strange grumblings and gruntings, peculiar noises which might have been speech. The mist thinned a fraction and Corum saw the outline of lumbering, malformed beasts, a wicker chariot. He had to peer upward to see the faint outline of the one who rode in the chariot. He saw reddish fur, saw an eight-fingered hand, all gnarled and covered in warts, clutching what appeared to be a monstrous hammer, but the shoulders and the head were completely obscured. Then the creaking battle-cart had gone past the window and silence came again to the street.

Corum wrapped the Sidhi cloak about his body. It seemed to have been made for a much larger man, for its folds completely engulfed him.

And then it seemed, to his astonishment, that he saw two rooms, as if his eyes were slightly out of focus. Yet the rooms were subtly different. One was the room of death in which Jhary sat huddled in his blankets and one was light, airy, full of sunshine.

And Corum understood, then, the properties of the Sidhi cloak. It had been long since he had been able to shift his body from one plane into another. Effectively this was what the mantle had done for him. Like Hy-Breasail, it was not completely of this plane; it moved him sideways, as it were, through the dimensions separating one plane from another.

'What has happened?' said Jhary-a-Conel peering in Corum's direction.

'Why? Have I vanished?'

Jhary shook his head. 'No,' he said, 'but you have become a little shadowy, as if the mist thickens around you.'

Corum frowned. 'So the cloak does not work, after all. I should have tested it before I left Caer Mahlod.'

Jhary-a-Conel looked thoughtful. 'Perhaps it will deceive Mabden eyes, Corum. You forget that I am used to travelling between the realms. But those who cannot see, who have no knowledge such as we possess, perhaps they will not see you.'

Corum made a bitter smile. 'Well,' he said, 'we must hope so, Jhary!'

He turned towards the door.

'Go warily, Corum,' said Jhary-a-Conel. 'Gaynor – the Fhoi Myore themselves – many are not of this world at all. Some may see you clearly. Others may gain just an impression of your outline. But there is much danger in what you plan.'

And Corum said nothing in reply but left the room and entered the street and began to move towards the tower by the river with a steady, dogged stride, as a man might go bravely to his inevitable death.

2. A HIGH KING
BROUGHT LOW

He stood directly in Corum's path as Corum went through the open gateway and began to ascend the gently rising steps which led to the entrance of the tall granite tower. He was big, barrel-chested, clad in leather, and in each white hand he held a cutlass. His red eyes glared. His bloodless lips curved in something which could have been a smile or a snarl.

Corum had met his kind before. This was one of the Fhoi Myore's living dead vassals, called the Ghoolegh. Often they rode as huntsmen with the Hounds of Kerenos, for they were drawn from the ranks of those who had been foresters before the Fhoi Myore came.

This must be the test, thought Corum. He stood less than a foot from the red-eyed Ghoolegh and assumed a martial position, one hand on his sword.

But the Goolegh did not respond. He continued to stare through Corum and plainly could not see him.

In some relief, his faith in the Sidhi cloak restored, Corum passed around the Ghoolegh guard and continued until he reached the entrance to the tower itself.

Here stood two more Ghoolegh and they were as unaware of Corum's presence as their fellow. He was almost cheerful as he walked through and began to mount the curving stairway leading up into the heart of the tower. The tower was wide and roughly square in shape. The steps were old and worn and the walls on both sides were either painted or carved with pictures of exceptionally beautiful workmanship. As with most Mabden art, they depicted famous deeds, great heroes, love stories and the doings of gods and demigods, yet they had a purity of conception, a beauty, which showed none of the darker aspects of superstition and religiosity. The metaphorical content of the old stories was completely understood by these Mabden and appreciated for what it was.

Here and there were the remains of tapestries which had been torn from the walls. Frost-coated, mist-rotted, it was possible to see that they had been of immeasurable value, worked in gold and silver thread as well as rich scarlets, yellows and blues. Corum mourned at the destruction the Fhoi Myore and their minions had wrought.

He reached the first storey of the tower and found himself on a wide stone-flagged landing, almost a room in itself, with benches lined along the walls and decorative shields set above them. And from one of the rooms off this landing he heard voices.

Confident now in the powers of his cloak he approached the half-open door and to his surprise felt warmth issuing from it. He was grateful for the warmth, but puzzled, too. Becoming more cautious, he peered round the door and was shocked.

Two figures sat beside a big fire which had been built in the stone hearth. Both were swathed in layers of thick, white fur. Both wore fur gauntlets. Both had no business being in Caer Llud at all. On the other side of the room food was being set out by a girl who had the same white flesh and red eyes of the Ghoolegh guards and was doubtless, like them, one of the living dead. It meant that the two by the fire were not in Caer Llud illicitly. They were obviously guests, with servants put at their disposal.

One of these guests of the Fhoi Myore was a tall, slender Mabden with jewelled rings on his gloved hands, a jewelled, golden collar at his throat. His long hair and his long beard were both grey, framing a handsome, old face. And worn by a thong passed over his head so that it rested upon his chest was a horn. It was a long horn and there were bands of silver and gold around it. Corum knew that every one of those bands represented a different forest beast. The Mabden was the one he had met near Moidel's Mount and with whom he had traded a cloak – a cloak in exchange for the horn which the Mabden

57

had, apparently recovered. It was the wizard Calatin, who planned secret plans which had nothing to do with loyalty either to his Mabden countrymen or their Fhoi Myore enemies – or so Corum had thought.

But still more shocking to Corum was the sight of the wizard's companion – the one who had sworn he would never involve himself in the affairs of the world. And this man must truly be a renegade, for it was the one who was self-called a dwarf yet was eight feet tall and at least four feet broad at the shoulder. Who had the fine, sensitive features which marked him as a cousin to the Vadhagh, for all that much of those features were covered in black hair. There was a glimpse of an iron breastplate beneath his many furs, there were polished iron greaves with gold inlays on his legs and he wore an iron polished helmet of similar workmanship. Beside him stood his huge double-bladed war-axe, not unlike Corum's axe, but much larger.

This was Goffanon, the Sidhi smith, of Hy-Breasail, who had given Corum the spear Bryionak and the bag of spittle which Calatin had wanted. How could Goffanon possibly have allied himself with the Fhoi Myore, let alone the wizard Calatin? Goffanon had sworn that he would never again involve himself in the wars between mortals and the Gods of Limbo! Had he deceived Corum? Had he been in league with the Fhoi Myore and the wizard Calatin all along? Yet, if so, why had he given Corum the spear Bryionak which had led to the defeat of the Fhoi Myore at Caer Mahlod?

Now, as if he sensed Corum's presence, Goffanon slowly began to turn his head towards the door and Corum withdrew hastily, not sure if the Sidhi would be able to see him.

There was something strange about Goffanon's face, something dull and tragic, but Corum had not had enough time to study the expression closely enough to be able to analyse it.

With heavy heart, horrified by Goffanon's treachery (though not over-surprised by Calatin's decision to league himself with the Fhoi Myore), Corum tiptoed back to the landing, hearing Calatin say:

'We shall go with them tomorrow when they march.'

And he heard Goffanon reply in a deep, distant voice:

'Now begins in earnest the conquest of the West.'

So the Fhoi Myore did prepare for battle and almost certainly they marched against Caer Mahlod again. And this time they had a Sidhi as an ally and there were no Sidhi weapons to thwart their ambitions.

Corum moved with greater urgency up the next stairway and had gone half-way when he turned a bend and saw a lump squatting so that it filled the whole stair and afforded him no room through which he could pass undetected.

The lump did not see him, but it lifted its snout and sniffed. Its three eyes, of disparate size, had a puzzled look. Its pink, bristle-covered flesh quivered as it pushed itself into a sitting position on its five arms. Three of the arms were human, though seemed to have belonged to a woman, a youth and an old man. One of the arms was simian, that of a gorilla, and one of the arms seemed to have been the property of some kind of large reptile. The legs which the lump now revealed were short and ended in a human foot, a cloven hoof and a dog-like paw respectively. The lump was naked, apparently sexless, and it was unarmed. It stank of excrement and of sweat and of corrupting food. It wheezed as it altered its position.

As silently as possible, Corum drew his sword as the three lids closed over the three mismatched eyes as the lump, seeing nothing, resettled itself to sleep again.

As the eyes closed Corum struck.

He struck through the oval mouth, through the roof of the mouth, into the brain. He knew that he could strike only once effectively before the lump made a noise which would bring other guards.

The eyes opened and instantly one closed again in a kind of obscene wink.

The others stared at the blade of the sword in astonishment, for it seemed to protrude from the thin air. The simian hand came up to touch the blade but it never completed the gesture. The hand fell limply back. The remaining eyes closed and Corum was sheathing his sword and clambering over the fat, yielding flesh as fast as he could, praying that none should find the lump's corpse before he had discovered the where-abouts of the Archdruid Amergin.

There were two Ghoolegh guards, their cutlasses at attention across their chests, at the top of this particular stair, but it was plain that they had heard nothing.

Hurriedly Corum slipped past them and mounted the next flight and there, on the landing above him, he saw two huge hounds, the largest of all the Hounds of Kerenos he had ever seen.

5

And these hounds were sniffing the air. They could not see him, but they had caught his scent. Both were voicing soft, deep growls.

Acting as rapidly as he had acted when he had seen the lump, Corum ran through the gap between the dogs and had the satisfaction of seeing them snap at the air and almost close their fangs on each other's throats.

And here was a great archway filled by a door of beaten bronze on which had been raised motifs of beautiful complexity. King Fiachadh had described it. This was the door to Amergin's apartments. And hanging on a brass hook beside the door, behind the head of one gigantic Ghoolegh guard, was a single iron key. And this was the key to the beautiful bronze door.

Behind Corum the Hounds of Kerenos, ordered not to leave their position, were whining and sniffing at the flagstones near where they sat. The Ghoolegh guard's dull features became curious. He lurched forward.

'What is it, dogs? Do strangers come?'

Corum stepped behind the Goolegh and silently drew the key from its hook, inserting it into the lock, turning it, opening the door and closing it behind him. With the distraction of the dogs to occupy his slow brain, the Ghoolegh might not notice the absence of the iron key.

Corum found himself in an apartment full of rich, dark hangings. He sniffed and was surprised to recognize the smell of new-cut grass. The apartment was warm, too, heated by a fire even larger than the one at which Calatin and Goffanon sat two floors below.

But where was Amergin?

Stealthily Corum crept from one dark room to another, his hand on his sword, expecting some new trap.

And then, at last, he saw something. At first he took it for an animal, for it was upon all fours and eating from a golden tray piled high with the strands of some vegetable.

The head turned but the eyes did not see Corum, still draped in his Sidhi mantle. Large, soft eyes stared at nothing and the jaws moved slowly as they chewed the vegetation. The body was clothed in sheepskin garments with the wool still on them. The wool was dirty and full of filthy scraps of thistle, briar and burrs as if torn from the body of a wild mountain sheep. Jacket, shirt and leggings were all of the same coarse stuff and there was even a hood of sheepskin drawn around the head, exposing only the face. The man looked ridiculous and pathetic and Corum knew that this was Amergin, High King of the Mabden, Archdruid of Craig Dôn, and that he was truly under a glamour.

It had been a handsome face, possibly an intelligent face, but now it was neither. The eyes stared unblinking into nothing, the jaws continued to chew at the grass.

Corum murmured: 'Amergin?'

And Amergin ceased his chewing. He opened his mouth and he uttered a single, frightened bleat.

He began to crawl towards the shadows where doubtless he thought he would find security.

Sadly, Corum drew his sword.

3. A TRAITOR SLEEPS, A FRIEND AWAKES

Without hesitation, Corum reversed his grip upon his sword and brought the round pommel down hard on the back of Amergin's neck, then he picked up the body, surprised by its lightness. The man was slowly starving to death on the diet of grass he had been fed. Corum had been told that there would be little chance of releasing Amergin from his enchantment until they were far away from Caer Llud. He would have to carry the Archdruid to safety.

Somehow he managed to drape his mantle over Amergin's body as well as his own, checking in a mirror that both he and Amergin were invisible. Looking once around the room he turned and walked back to the bronze door, his sword still in his hand, though also covered by his mantle.

Cautiously he turned the key and opened the door. The Ghoolegh was standing up, close to the hounds. Both the devil dogs remained nervous, suspicious, but were still seated, their heads coming almost to the Ghoolegh's shoulder. The red, stupid eyes of the guard peered first down the stair and then about the landing and Corum was sure that he had seen the door closing, but then he looked again down the stairs and Corum was able to replace the key on its hook.

But he moved hastily. The key clinked against the stone of the wall. The dogs pricked up their ears. They snarled. Standing at the top of the stairs the Ghoolegh began to turn. Corum rushed forward and kicked the Ghoolegh off-balance. The undead creature yelled and fell, tumbling head over heels down the granite steps. The dogs glared and one snapped at Corum, but the Vadhagh prince lunged forward with his sword and cut through the hound's jugular as cleanly as he had slain the lump.

Then he felt a blow on his back and staggered, taking two involuntary bounds down the stairs and only barely managing to keep his balance, burdened as he was by the unconscious High King, staggering round as the remaining hound leapt from the top of the stair, its red jaws extended, its glistening yellow fangs dripping saliva, its fur bristling, its forelegs extended, and Corum only had time to bring up his sword before those gigantic paws had struck his chest and he was driven back against the wall, glimpsing from the corner of his single eye two Ghoolegh guards running to discover the cause of the commotion.

But his sword point had found the hound's heart and the beast had been dead even as it struck Corum. He dragged himself from under it, keeping a firm hold on Amergin, tugging his sword from the hound's corpse and then rearranging the Sidhi mantle about his body.

The Ghoolegh had seen something and they hesitated. They looked at the corpse of the hound, they looked at each other, uncertain what to do. Corum drew back, permitting himself a relieved grin as the Ghoolegh brandished their cutlasses and began to ascend the steps, plainly believing that whoever had slain the hound was still above.

Down the next flight Corum ran, clambering over the undetected corpse of the lump, down the rest of the steps until, panting, he reached the landing.

But Calatin and Goffanon had heard the sounds of strife and they were coming out of their room. Calatin was first. He was shouting.

'What is it? Who attacks?' He stared straight through Corum.

Corum made to move forward.

Then Goffanon said in a thick, slurred voice which had more curiosity in it than anger:

'Corum! What do you in Caer Llud?'

Corum made to put a finger to his lips, hoping that Goffanon still had some loyalties to his Vadhagh cousin. Certainly Goffanon's great axe was still held loosely in his hand. He did not seem prepared to do battle.

'Corum?' Calatin whirled from where he stood on the first step. 'Where?'

'There,' said Goffanon pointing.

Calatin understood swiftly. 'Invisible! He must be slain. Slay him! Slay him, Goffanon!'

'Very well.' Goffanon began to get a grip on the haft of his axe.

'Goffanon! Traitor!' yelled Corum, and put up his own sword, revealing his position to Calatin who took a dagger from his belt and began to move towards him.

Goffanon was moving slowly, as if drugged. Corum decided to deal with Calatin first. He whirled his sword round in a poorly considered stroke which yet found Calatin's head and downed him, but the wizard was only knocked senseless by the flat of the sword. Corum gave Goffanon all his concentration, wishing desperately that he was not hampered by the burden of Amergin across his shoulder.

'Corum?' Goffanon frowned. 'Must I kill you?'

'It's no wish of mine, traitor.'

Goffanon began to lower his axe. 'But what does Calatin wish?'

'He wishes nothing.' Corum believed that he understood a little now of Goffanon's position. Amergin was not the only occupant of the tower under a glamour. 'He wishes you to protect me. That is what he wants. He wishes that you come with me.'

'Very well,' said Goffanon simply. And he fell in beside Corum.

'Hurry.'

Corum stooped to wrench something from Calatin's body. From above came the puzzled voices of the Ghoolegh and the Ghoolegh whom Corum had pushed down the steps was beginning to slither forward, though almost every bone must have been broken. They were hard to slay, those who were already dead.

'Those beyond the tower must soon realize that something is afoot here.'

They began to descend the last stairway.

There was a noise below and round the bend came the remaining Ghoolegh while at the same time Corum heard their comrades rushing down the steps, having decided that their enemies must somehow have escaped them.

Two above and three below. The Ghoolegh hesitated, seeing

only Goffanon. Doubtless they had been told that Goffanon was not an enemy and this confused them further. As quickly as he could, Corum crept past those who blocked the path below and, as they began to climb towards Goffanon he did the only thing he could do against the living dead, he cut at the tendons of their legs so that they flopped down, using their arms to continue to crawl towards Goffanon, their cutlasses still in their hands. Goffanon turned with his axe and chopped at the legs of the two remaining Ghoolegh, severing those limbs. No blood spouted as the guards collapsed.

Then they were through the door, running into the cold, poisoned mist, down the steps from the tower, through the gateway, into the freezing streets, Goffanon loping beside Corum, keeping pace with him, his brows still drawn together as if in tremendous concentration.

Into the house they went and Jhary-a-Conel was already mounted, swathed still in coarse blankets so that only his face peeped through, holding Corum's horse ready for him. Jhary was astonished to see the Sidhi smith.

'Are you Amergin?'

But Corum was tearing the mantle of invisibility from him, revealing the starved figure in old sheepskins who lay over his shoulder.

'This is Amergin,' he explained curtly. 'The other's a cousin of mine I thought a traitor.' Corum heaved the prone Archdruid over his saddle, speaking to Goffanon. 'Do you come with us, Sidhi? Or do you remain to serve the Fhoi Myore?'

'Serve the Fhoi Myore? A Sidhi would not do that! Goffanon serves nobody!' The speech was still thick, the eyes still dull.

Having no time to waste either upon analyzing the cause of Goffanon's strange actions or conversing with the great Smith to learn more, Corum said roughly:

'Then come with us from Caer Llud.'

'Aye,' said Goffanon musingly. 'I would prefer to leave Caer Llud.'

They rode through the chilling mist, avoiding the massing of warriors on the far side of the city. Perhaps it was this which had allowed them to enter the city and leave it without detection – the Fhoi Myore thought only of their wars upon the West and gathered all their forces, all their attention, together for this single venture.

Whatever the reason, they were soon able to leave the outskirts of Caer Llud and were riding up a snow-covered hill, with the Dwarf Goffanon running easily beside their horses, his axe upon his shoulder, his beard and hair streaming behind him, his huge breath billowing in the air.

'Gaynor will soon understand what has happened and be most angry,' Corum told Jhary-a-Conel. 'He will realize that he has made a fool of himself. We can expect pursuit soon and he will be most vicious if he finds us.'

Jhary peered out from under his many blankets, refusing to relinquish a morsel of warmth.

'We must make speed for Craig Dôn,' he said. 'There we will have time to consider what to do next.' He managed to grin. 'At least we now have something the Fhoi Myore wish to keep – we have Amergin.'

'Aye. They'll be reluctant to destroy us if it means destroying Amergin too. But we cannot rely on that.' Corum adjusted the body more securely across his saddle.

'From what I know of the Fhoi Myore, they'll not think oversubtly upon the matter,' agreed Jhary.

'Always our good luck and our bad luck both, the mentality of the Fhoi Myore!' Corum grinned back at his old friend. 'For all that there is much danger ahead of us, Jhary-a-Conel, I cannot but feel right well satisfied with today's accomplishments. Not long since I knew I went to my death, my quest unfulfilled. Now should I die, at least I shall know that I was partially successful!'

'It will not give me much satisfaction, however,' said Jhary-a-Conel feelingly. And he looked over his shoulder to Caer Llud in the distance as if he already heard the baying of the Hounds of Kerenos.

They left the mist behind and the air became relatively warmer. Jhary began to strip the blankets from him and drop them behind him in the snow as they galloped on. The horses needed no urging this time. They were as glad to be free of Caer Llud and its unnatural mist as were their riders.

It was four days before they heard the noise of the hounds.

And Craig Dôn was still some distance off.

4. OF ENCHANTMENTS AND OMENS

'Of the few things I fear,' said Goffanon, 'I fear those dogs most.'

Since they had left Caer Llud far behind them, his speech had become increasingly coherent, his mind sharper, though he had said little about his association with the wizard Calatin.

'There must be still thirty miles of hard country before Craig Dôn is reached.'

They had come to a stop upon a hill, searching through the dancing snow for signs of the dogs which pursued them.

Corum was thoughtful. He looked at Amergin who had woken the night after they had fled Caer Llud and had since been bound to stop his straying. Occasionally the High King would utter a bleat, but it was impossible to divine what he wanted from them, unless it was to indicate his hunger, for he had eaten little since they had fled the city. He spent most of his time in sleep and even when he was awake he was passive, resigned.

Corum said to Goffanon:

'Why were you in Caer Llud? I remember you telling me you intended to spend the rest of your days in Hy-Breasail. Did Calatin come to the Enchanted Isle and offer you a bargain which attracted you?'

Goffanon snorted. 'Calatin? Come to Hy-Breasail? Of course not. And what bargain could he offer me that was better than

67

that which you offered? No, I fear that you were the instrument of my alliance with the Mabden wizard.'

'I? How?'

'Remember how I scoffed at Calatin's superstitions? Remember how thoughtlessly I spat into that little bag you gave me? Well, Calatin had a good reason for wanting that spittle. He has more power than I guessed – and a power I barely understand. It was the dryness which first came upon me, you see. No matter how much I drank I still felt thirsty – terrible, painful thirst. My mouth was forever dry, Corum. I was dying of thirst, though I near drained the rivers and streams of my island, gulping down the water as fast as I could, yet never satisfying that thirst. I was horrified – and I was dying. Then came a vision – a vision sent by that man of power, Corum, by that Mabden. And the vision spoke to me and told me that Hy-Breasail was rejecting me as it rejected the Mabden, that I should die if I remained there – die of this frightful thirst.'

The dwarf shrugged his huge shoulders. 'Well, I debated this, but I was already mad with thirst. At last I set sail for the mainland, where Calatin greeted me. He gave me something to drink. That drink did satisfy my thirst. But it also robbed me of my senses and put me completely in the wizard's power. I became his slave. He can still reach out for me. He could still trap me again and make me do his bidding. While he has that charm he made from my spittle – the charm which brings on the thirst – he can also control my thoughts to a large extent – he can somehow occupy my mind and cause my body to perform certain actions. And while he occupies my mind, I am not responsible for what I do.'

'So by delivering that blow to Calatin's head, I was able to break his influence over you?'

'Yes. And by the time he recovered we were doubtless beyond the range of his magic-working.' Goffanon sighed. 'I had never thought a Mabden could command such mysterious gifts.'

'And that is how the horn came back in Calatin's keeping?'

'Aye. I gained nothing from my bargain with you, Corum.'

Corum smiled as he drew something from beneath his cloak.

'Nothing,' he said. 'But I gained something from that most recent encounter.'

'My horn!'

'Well,' said Corum, 'I remember how mercenary you were, friend Goffanon, in the matter of bargains. Strictly speaking, I would say this horn is mine.'

Goffanon nodded his great head philosophically. 'That is fair,' he said. 'Very well, the horn is yours, Corum. I lost it, after all, through my own stupidity.'

'But through my unconscious connivance,' said Corum. 'Let me borrow the horn a while, Goffanon. When the time seems ripe, I will return it to you.'

'It is a better bargain than I made with you, Corum. I feel shamed.'

'Well, Goffanon, what do you plan to do? Return to Hy-Breasail?'

Goffanon shook his head.

'What should I gain by that? It seems my best interests lie with your cause, Corum, for if you defeat Calatin and the Fhoi Myore, then I am freed from Calatin's service forever. If I return to my island, Calatin can always find me again.'

'Then you are fully with us?'

'Aye.'

Jhary-a-Conel shifted nervously in his saddle. 'Listen,' he said, 'they come much closer now. I think they have our scent. I think we are in considerable danger, my friends.'

But Corum was laughing. 'I think not, Jhary-a-Conel. Not now.'

'Why so? Listen to their ghastly baying!' His lips curled in distaste. 'The wolves seek the sheep, eh?'

And, as if in confirmation, Amergin bleated softly.

Then Corum laughed. 'Let them come closer,' he said. 'The closer the better.'

He knew that it was wrong to leave Jhary in such suspense but he was enjoying the sensation – so often had Jhary made mysteries himself.

They rode on.

And all the while the Hounds of Kerenos came closer.

They were in sight of Craig Dôn by the time the hounds appeared behind them, but they knew that the devil dogs could move faster than could they. There was no chance at all of reaching the seven stone circles before the hounds caught them.

Corum peered backward at their pursuers, looking for signs of a suit of armour which constantly shifted its colours, but there was none. White faces, red eyes – the Ghoolegh huntsmen controlled the pack. They were most expert at doing so, having been slaves of the Fhoi Myore for generations, bred beyond the sea in eastern lands before the Fhoi Myore began their re-conquest of the west. Gaynor, no doubt against his will, had been needed by the Fhoi Myore to lead the marching warriors who went against Caer Mahlod (if that was where they went) and so had been kept from the pursuit. This was just as well, thought Corum, unslinging the horn and putting its ornamental mouthpiece to his lips. He took a deep breath.

'Ride for Craig Dôn,' he told the others. 'Goffanon, take Amergin.'

The smith drew the limp body of the Archdruid from Corum's saddle and swung it easily over his massive shoulder.

'But you will die . . . ' Jhary began.

'I will not,' said Corum. 'Not if I am careful in what I do now. Go. Goffanon will tell you the properties of this horn.'

'Horns!' Jhary exclaimed. 'I am sick of them. Horns for bringing the apocalypse, horns for calling demons – now horns for handling dogs! The gods grow unimaginative!' And with that peculiar observation he kicked his heels into the flanks of his horse and rode rapidly towards the tall stones of Craig Dôn, Goffanon loping behind him.

And Corum blew the horn once and though the Hounds of Kerenos pricked up their red, tufted ears, they still came running towards their quarry – running in a great pack made up of at least two score dogs. The Ghoolegh, mounted on pale horses, were, however, unsure. Corum could see that they hung back, where normally they would have chased behind the dogs.

Now the Hounds of Kerenos yelled in glee as they had Corum's scent and, veering slightly, sped towards him through the snow.

And Corum blew the horn a second time and the yellow eyes of the hounds, so close, so glaring, took on a somewhat puzzled expression.

Now other horns shouted as the Ghoolegh called their dogs off in panic, for they knew what would happen to them if the horn sounded a third time.

The Hounds of Kerenos were so near to Corum now that he could smell their stinking, steaming breath.

And suddenly they stopped in their tracks, whined and began reluctantly to trot back across the wind-blown snow to where the Ghoolegh waited.

And when the Hounds of Kerenos were in retreat, Corum blew the horn a third time.

He saw the Ghoolegh clutch their heads. He saw the Ghoolegh fall from their saddles. And he knew that they were dead, for the third blast of that horn always killed them – it was the punishing blast with which Kerenos slew those who failed to obey him.

The Hounds of Kerenos, whose last instructions had been to return, continued to lope back to where the dead Ghoolegh lay. And Corum whistled to himself as he tucked the horn into his belt and made for the Craig Dôn at an almost leisurely gait.

'Perhaps it is sacrilege, but it is a convenient place to put him while we debate the problem.' Jhary looked down at Amergin who lay upon the great altar stone within the inner circle of columns.

It was dark. A fire burned fitfully.

'I cannot understand why he eats only the few pieces of fruit or vegetables we brought. It is as if his innards have become sheep's innards, too. If this continues, Corum, we shall deliver a dead High King to Caer Mahlod!'

'You spoke earlier of being able to reach through to his inner mind,' Corum said. 'Is that possible? If so, we can learn what to do to help him, perhaps.'

'Aye, with the aid of my little cat I might be able to do that, but it will take much time and considerable energy. I would eat before I begin.'

'By all means.'

And then Jhary-a-Conel ate, and he fed his cat almost as much food as he consumed himself, while Corum and Goffanon ate only sparingly and poor Amergin ate nothing at all, for their supplies of dried fruit and vegetables were almost gone.

The moon peered for a moment through the clouds and it struck the altar with its rays and the costume of sheepskin gleamed. Then the moon went away again and the only light came from the flickering fire which flung red shadows among the old stones.

Jhary-a-Conel whispered to his cat. He stroked his cat and the cat purred. Slowly, the cat in his arms, he began to approach the altar where starved, wasted Amergin lay, breathing shallow breaths as he slept.

Jhary-a-Conel put the little winged cat's head against the head of Amergin and then he drew his own head down so that it touched the other side of the cat's head. Silence fell.

There came a bleating, loud and urgent, and it was impossible

71

for the watchers to judge whether it came from Amergin's mouth, from the cat's, or from Jhary's.

The bleating died away.

It became darker as, untended, the fire died. Corum could see the dirty white form of Amergin upon the altar, the faint outline of the cat as it pressed its tiny skull to the High King's, the tense features of Jhary-a-Conel.

Jhary's voice:

'Amergin . . . Amergin . . . noble druid . . . pride of your folk . . . Amergin . . . Amergin . . . come back to us . . . '

Another bleat, this time wavering and unsure.

'Amergin . . . '

Corum remembered the calling which had summoned him from his own world, the world of the Vadhagh, to this world. Jhary's incantation was not unlike that of King Mannach. And possibly this had something to do with Amergin's enchantment: he lived a different life entirely, the life of a sheep, perhaps in a world which was not quite this one. And if that were the case his 'real' self might be reached. Corum could not begin to understand what the people of this world called magic, but he knew something of the multiverse with its variety of planes which sometimes intersected and he believed that their power probably derived from some half-conscious knowledge of these Realms.

'Amergin, High King . . . Amergin, Archdruid . . . '

The bleating became fainter and at the same time seemed to assume the qualities of human speech.

'Amergin . . . '

There was a catlike mewl, a distant voice which could have come from any one of the three upon the altar.

'Amergin of the family of Amergin . . . the knowledge-seekers . . . '

'Amergin.' This was Jhary's voice, strained and strange. 'Amergin. Do you understand your fate?'

'An enchantment . . . I am no longer a man. . . . Why should this displease me . . . ?'

'Because your own folk need your guidance, your strength, your presence amongst them!'

'I am all things . . . we are all of us all things . . . it is immaterial, the form we take . . . the spirit . . . '

'Sometimes it is important, Amergin. As now, when the fate of the whole Mabden folk rests upon your assuming your

72

former role. What will bring you back to your folk, Amergin? What power will restore you to them?'

'*Only the power of the Oak and the Ram. Only the Oak Woman can call me home. If it matters to you that I return, then find the Golden Oak and the Silvern Ram, find one who understands their properties. . . . Only – the Oak Woman – can – call me – home . . .*'

And then there came the agitated bleating of a sheep and Jhary fell back from the altar and the cat spread its wings and flew away to perch high on top of one of the great stone arches, crouching there as if in fear.

And the wind's melancholy voice came from the distance and the clouds seemed to grow darker in the sky and the bleating of a sheep filled the stone circle and then died away.

Goffanon was the first to speak, tugging at the hairs of his black beard, his voice a growl:

'The Oak and the Ram. Two of what the Mabden term their "Treasures" – Sidhi gifts, both. It seems to me that I recall something of them. One of the Mabden who came to my island spoke of them before he died.' Goffanon shrugged. 'Yet most Mabden who came to my island spoke of such things. It was their interest in talismans and spells which brought them to Hy-Breasail.'

'What did he say?' Corum asked.

'Well, he told the tale of the lost Treasures – how the old warrior Onragh fled with them from Caer Llud and how they were scattered. These two were lost close to the borders of the land of the Tuha-na-Gwyddneu Garanhir, which is north of the land of the Tuha-na-Cremm Croich, across a sea – though there is a way by land, also. One of that folk found the Golden Oak and the Silvern Ram – large talismans both, of fine Sidhi workmanship – and took them back to his folk where they were held in great reverence and where, for all I know, they still are.'

'So we must seek the Oak and the Ram before we can restore Amergin to his senses,' said Jhary-a-Conel. He looked pale and exhausted. 'Yet I fear he will die before we can achieve that. He needs nourishment and the only nourishment which will keep him properly alive is that grass which the Fhoi Myore vassals fed him. It is a grass containing certain magical agents which, while they kept him firmly under his enchantment, also supplied his body's primary needs. Unless he is restored to his human identity shortly, he will die, my friends.'

Jhary-a-Conel spoke flatly and neither Corum nor Goffanon

needed to convince themselves of the truth of his words. It was evident, for one thing, that Amergin was beginning to waste away, particularly since their supplies of fruit and vegetables were all but gone.

'Yet we must go to the land of the Tuha-na-Gwyddneu Garanhir if we are to find those things which will save him,' said Corum. 'And he will surely die before we reach that land. It seems that we are defeated.'

He looked down at the pathetic sleeping figure of he who had once been the symbol of Mabden pride. 'We sought to save the High King. Instead, we have slain him.'

5. DREAMS AND DECISIONS

Corum dreamed of a field of sheep; a pleasant scene, save when all the sheep looked up at once and had the faces of men and women he had known.

He dreamed that he ran for the safety of his old home, Castle Erorn by the sea, but when he neared it he found that a great chasm had fallen between him and the entrance to the castle. He dreamed that he blew upon a horn and that this horn called all the gods to the Earth and the Earth became the field of their final battle. And he was consumed by an enormous sense of guilt, recalling many deeds which Corum awake could never recall: tragic deeds; the murder of friends and lovers, the betrayal of races, the destruction of the weak and of the innocent. And while a small voice reminded him that he had also destroyed the strong and the evil in his long career through a thousand incarnations, he was not consoled, for now he recalled Amergin and soon he would have Amergin's death upon his conscience. Once again his idealism had led to the destruction of another soul and he could not reconcile his tortured spirit.

And now gleeful music began to sound; mocking music, sweet music – the music of a harp.

And Corum turned from the chasm and he saw three figures standing there. One of the figures he recognized with pleasure. It was Medhbh, lovely Medhbh, in a smock of blue samite, with her red hair braided and bracelets of red gold upon her arms and ankles, a sword in one hand and a sling in the other. He smiled at her, but she did not return his smile. The figure next to her he also recognized now and he recognized that figure with horror. It was a youth whose flesh shone with the colour of pale gold. A youth who smiled without kindness and played upon the mocking harp.

Corum dreamed that he made to draw his sword, moving to attack the youth with the flesh of gold, but then the third figure advanced, raising a hand. This figure was the most shadowy of the three and Corum realized that he feared it more than he feared the youth with the harp, though he could not see the face at all. He saw that the raised hand was of silver and that the cloak the figure wore was of scarlet and then he turned his back again in horror, not daring to look upon the face because he was afraid he would see his own face there.

And Corum leapt into the chasm while the music of the harp grew louder and louder, more and more triumphant, and he fell through a night which had no ending.

And then there was a blinding whiteness which swallowed him and he realized that he had opened his eyes upon the dawn.

Slowly the great stones of Craig Dôn came into focus, dark and grim against the snow which surrounded them. He felt something gripping him and he tried to struggle free, fearing that Gaynor had found him, but then he heard Goffanon's deep voice saying:

'It is over, Corum. You are awake.'

Corum gasped. 'Such dreadful dreams, Goffanon . . . '

'What else did you expect if you sleep at the centre of Craig Dôn?' growled the Sidhi dwarf. 'Particularly after witnessing Jhary-a-Conel's work of last night.'

'It was similar to a dream I had when I first came to Hy-Breasail,' Corum said, rubbing at his frozen face and taking deep breaths of cold air as if he hoped thus to dispel the memory of the dreams.

'Because Hy-Breasail has similar properties to Craig Dôn, there is every reason why your dreams should be the same,' said Goffanon. He rose, his great bulk looming over Corum. 'Though some have pleasant dreams at Craig Dôn, and others have magnificent, inspiring dreams, I'm told.'

'I have need of such dreams at present,' said Corum.

Goffanon shifted his war-axe from his right hand to his left and offered the free hand to Corum who took it and let the

Sidhi smith help him to his feet. Amergin still slept upon the altar, covered by a cloak, and Jhary slept near the ashes of the fire, his cat curled up close to his face.

'We must go to the land of the Tuha-na-Gwyddneu Garanhir,' said Goffanon. 'I have been considering the problem.'

Corum smiled with his frozen lips. 'You league yourself fully with our cause, then?'

Goffanon shrugged with poor grace.

'It seems so. I've little choice. To reach that land we must go part of the way by sea. It will be the quickest way of making the journey.'

'But we are much burdened,' said Corum, 'and will make slow progress with Amergin.'

'Then one of us must take Amergin to the relative safety of Caer Mahlod,' said Goffanon, 'while the others make the longer journey to Caer Garanhir. Returning by sea, assuming that we have succeeded in finding the Golden Oak and the Silvern Ram, we should be able to get to Caer Mahlod with relative ease. It is the only way we have, if Amergin is to have even the faintest hope of living.'

'Then it is the way we must take,' said Corum simply.

Jhary-a-Conel had begun to stir. A hand reached out and found a wide-brimmed hat, cramming it on his head. He sat up, blinking. The cat made a small, complaining noise and curled itself sleepily upon his lap while Jhary stretched and rubbed at his eyes.

'How is Amergin?' he said. 'I dreamed of him. He led a great gathering here, at Craig Dôn, and all the Mabden spoke with a single voice. It was a fine dream.'

'Amergin still sleeps,' said Corum. And he told Jhary what he and Goffanon had discussed.

Jhary nodded his agreement. 'But which of us is to take Amergin to Caer Mahlod?' He got to his feet, cradling the black and white cat in his arm. 'I think it should be me.'

'Why so?'

'A simple task, for one thing, to travel from this point to another and deliver our sheepish friend. Secondly, I play no important part in the destinies involved. The folk of Gwyddneu Garanhir are more likely to show respect for two Sidhi heroes than for one.'

'Very well,' Corum agreed, 'you shall ride with Amergin for Caer Mahlod and there tell them all that has taken place and all we intend to do. Warn them, too, that the Fhoi Myore come again. With Amergin within the walls of Caer Mahlod, they could be saved from Balahr's frigid gaze and time might be bought at a result. Happily the Fhoi Myore do not travel with particular swiftness and there is a chance we can return before they reach Caer Mahlod . . . '

'If they do, indeed, head for Caer Mahlod,' said Goffanon. 'We know only that they plan to march west. It could even be that Craig Dôn itself is their destination, that they have some idea of destroying the place.'

'Why do they fear it so?' Corum said. 'Have they, any longer, the need?'

Goffanon rubbed at his beard. 'Possibly,' he said. 'Craig Dôn was built by Sidhi and by Mabden both, at the time of our first great war with the Fhoi Myore. It was built according to certain metaphysical principles and it had several functions, both practical and symbolical. One of the practical functions was for it to act as a kind of trap which would swallow all the Fhoi Myore when they were lured here. It has the power – or, rather, it *had* the power – to restore those who do not belong in this Realm to the realms where they do belong. However, it does not work for the Sidhi or I should have departed this world long-since. It was our fate to accomplish its construction without being able to use it for our own ends. As it happened, we were not successful in luring all the Fhoi Myore here and ever since then those who survived have given the place wide clearance. There are rituals involved, too . . . '

Goffanon's expression became distant, as if he recalled the old days when he and all his brothers fought the might of the Fhoi Myore in their epic struggle. He looked out at the widening circles of stone columns.

'Aye,' he mused, 'this was a great place of power once, was Craig Dôn.'

Corum handed two things to Jhary-a-Conel. The first was the long, curved horn and the second was the Sidhi mantle.

'Take these,' he said, 'since you ride alone. The horn will protect you from the Hounds of Kerenos and the Ghoolegh huntsmen. The cloak will disguise you from the People of the Pines and others who pursue you. You will need both these things if you are to reach Caer Mahlod safely.'

'But what of you and Goffanon? Will you not need protection?'

Corum shook his head. 'We shall risk what we must risk. There are two of us and we are not burdened by Amergin.'

Jhary nodded. 'I accept the gifts, then.'

Soon they had mounted their horses and were riding through the stone arches, Goffanon running ahead with his war-axe upon his fur-clad shoulder, his helm of polished iron glinting in the cold light from the sky.

'Now you ride south-west and we ride north-west,' said Corum. 'Our ways will part soon, Jhary-a-Conel.'

'Let us pray they'll meet again.'

'Let us hope so.'

They spurred their horses and rode together for a while, enjoying one another's company but speaking little.

And a little later Corum watched from his motionless horse as Jhary rode rapidly for Caer Mahlod, his cloak billowing behind him, the semi-conscious figure of the enchanted High King tied across his horse's neck.

Far across the snow-shrouded plain rode Jhary-a-Conel, growing smaller and smaller and finally becoming obscured by a gust of wind-borne snow, blotted from Corum's sight but not from his thoughts.

Jhary and Jhary's fate was often in Corum's mind as he rode for the coast, the tireless Goffanon loping always beside him.

And sometimes, too, Corum would recall the dream he had dreamed at Craig Dôn, and then he would ride still harder, as if he hoped to leave such memories behind him.

6. A FLIGHT ACROSS THE WAVES

Corum wiped his forehead free from the sweat which clung to it and gratefully dropped his byrnie and his helm into the bottom of the small boat.

The sun was high in a cloudless sky and while the day was actually only as warm as a day in early spring it seemed to be almost tropically hot both to Corum and Goffanon who, in their ride to the coast, had become used to the aching cold of those lands conquered by the Fhoi Myore. Corum was clad now only in his shirt and his leggings, his sword and dirk strapped about his waist and the rest of his war-gear tied across the back of his horse. He was reluctant to leave the horse behind him, but there was no easy means of transporting it across the ocean which gleamed ahead. The boat they had found was barely large enough to take Goffanon's great bulk, let alone Corum's.

Corum stood on the quay of the abandoned fishing village and wondered if Fhoi Myore minions had come here or if the inhabitants had been among those who had fled to Caer Mahlod during the first invasion of the Cold Folk. Whatever the circumstances of their flight, they had left much behind them, including several small boats. The larger boats, Corum guessed, had been taken either to the land of the Tuha-na-Gwyddneu Garanhir or even further to the land of the Tuha-na-Manannan, King Fiachadh's land. There were none of the usual signs of wanton Fhoi Myore slaying. It was his belief that the folk of the village had been hasty in their decision to leave. The white houses, the gardens in which flowers and vegetables grew, all looked as if they were still occupied and tended. The flight must have been comparatively recent.

Gaffanon, complaining about the heat but refusing to remove his breastplate or war-cap, keeping, also, a firm grip on his double-headed axe, clambered from the short flight of stone steps and into the boat as Corum steadied it for him. Then Corum got cautiously into the bow and settled himself, laying his lance and his axe along the bottom of the boat and unshipping the oars (for Goffanon had insisted that he understood nothing of the art of rowing). Corum would dearly have given everything for a sail, but had been able to find nothing which would serve. He pushed off from the quay and manoeuvred the boat until his back was to the distant shoreline over the water, their destination. He began to row with long, strong strokes which at first wearied him but then, as he became used to the rhythm, involved seemingly less and less effort as Goffanon's weight increased their momentum through the clear, still waters of the sea.

The smell of the brine was good after the snow-laden air he had breathed so long and there was a sense of peace upon the sea which he had not known for a long while, even when he had sailed Calatin's boat for Hy-Breasail to meet (though he had not known it then) the huge self-styled dwarf who now sat in the stern and dangled a huge, heavily muscled hand in the water for all the world like a maiden being taken for a pleasure trip by her swain. Corum grinned, his liking for the Sidhi smith growing all the time.

'Perhaps at Caer Mahlod they will find herbs which will sustain Amergin,' said Goffanon, staring idly over the water as the coastline disappeared behind him. 'There, at least, they can grow such things. They grow in precious few parts of the old Mabden lands now.'

Corum, deciding to take a moment's rest from rowing, drew in the oars and drew a deep breath.

'Aye,' he said, 'it's what I hope. Yet if the grass Amergin ate at Caer Llud was specially treated it might be hard to find something matching it exactly. However,' he grinned, 'this sunshine makes me feel considerably more confident.' And he began to row again.

It was some time later that Goffanon spoke again. He drew his black brows together and peered over Corum's shoulder, looking beyond Corum in the direction in which they rowed. 'Sea-fog ahead, by the look of it. Strange to find it so isolated and in such weather . . . '

Corum, reluctant to interrupt the rhythm of his rowing, did not look back but continued his steady strokes.

'Thick, too,' said Goffanon some moments later. 'It would probably be best to avoid it.'

And now Corum did pause in his rowing and turn to look. Goffanon was right. The sea-fog was spreading across a huge area, almost completely obscuring the sight of the land ahead. And now that Corum ceased his exertions he felt that it had become subtly colder, for all that the sun continued to shine.

'Bad luck for us,' he said, 'but it will take too long to row around it. We'll risk rowing through and hope that it does not cover too wide an area.' And Corum rowed on.

But soon the cold had actually become uncomfortable and he rolled down his sleeves. Still this was not enough and he paused to draw his heavy byrnie over his body and place his helmet upon his head and this seemed to impair his rowing and it was as if he dipped his oars in clinging mud. Tendrils of mist began to move around the boat and Goffanon frowned again, and Goffanon shivered.

'Can it be?' he growled, shifting so that the boat rocked wildly and they were almost pitched into the sea. 'Can it be?'

'You think it Fhoi Myore mist?' Corum murmured.

'I think it resembles Fhoi Myore mist most closely.'

'I think so, too.'

Now the mist was all around them and they could see only a few yards in all directions. Corum stopped rowing altogether and the boat drifted slower and slower until suddenly it stopped altogether. Corum looked over the side.

The sea had frozen. It had frozen almost instantly, for the waves had become ridges and on some of those ridges were delicate patterns which could only have been foam.

Corum's spirits sank and it was with resignation and despair that he stood up in the boat and bent to pick up his lance and his axe.

Goffanon, too, rose and tentatively put a fur-booted foot upon the ice, testing it. He lumbered from the boat and stood upon the sea, tying the thongs of his fur cloak together so that he was completely covered. His breath began to steam. Corum followed suit, wrapping his own cloak around him, staring this way and that. He heard a noise in the far distance. A grunt. A shout. And perhaps he heard the creaking of a great wicker battle-cart, the heavy footfalls of some malformed beast upon the ice. Was it thus that the Fhoi Myore built their roads across the sea, needing no ships? Was this ice their version of a bridge? Or did they know that Goffanon and Corum came this way and sought to thwart their progress?

They would know soon, thought Corum as he crouched beside the boat and watched. The Fhoi Myore and their minions were moving from east to west, in the same direction as Corum and Goffanon but at a slightly different angle. In the dim distance Corum saw dark shapes riding and marching and sniffed the familiar scent of pines, saw the bulky shapes of Fhoi Myore chariot-riders, and once he glimpsed the flickering armour of one who could only be Gaynor. And now he began to realize that the Fhoi Myore marched not against Caer Mahlod at all but most likely against Caer Garanhir, which was their destination. And if the Fhoi Myore reached Caer Garanhir before them, the chances of finding the Oak and the Ram were very poor.

'Garanhir,' muttered Goffanon, 'they go to Garanhir.'

'Aye,' said Corum despairingly, 'and we have no choice now but to follow behind them, then hope to overtake them when they reach the land. We must warn Garanhir if we can. We must warn King Daffyn, Goffanon!'

Goffanon shrugged his massive shoulders and tugged at his shaggy black beard and rubbed his nose. Then he spread his left hand and raised his double-headed war-axe in his right hand and he smiled. 'Indeed, we must,' he said.

They were thankful that the Hounds of Kerenos did not run with the Fhoi Myore army. These, doubtless, still scoured the countryside about Craig Dôn, looking for the three friends and Amergin. They would have had no chance at all of avoiding detection if those dogs had been present. Moving warily, Corum and Goffanon skulked in the wake of the Fhoi Myore, peering ahead in the hope that they would soon sight the land. The going was difficult, for the waves had formed small hills and dangerous ruts in the frozen sea. They were exhausted by the time they witnessed the landing of the Fhoi Myore and the People of the Pines on shores which had, an hour since, been green and lush and which were suddenly ice-covered and dead.

And the sea began to melt as the Fhoi Myore passed and Corum and Goffanon found themselves wading through water which was still freezing and which rose to Corum's chin and Goffanon's chest.

And, as he stumbled up the frosty beach, his throat choked with a mixture of sea and mist, Corum felt himself seized, weapons and all, about the waist and he was moving headlong up a hillside, borne by Goffanon who was wasting no time, running easily with Corum under one arm, his beard and hair flying in the wind, his greaves and his armour rattling on his massive body, apparently in no way slowed by his burden.

Corum's ribs ached but he managed to remark: 'You are a most useful dwarf, Goffanon. I am amazed at the energy possessed by one of such small stature as yourself.'

'I suppose I compensate for my shortness by cultivating stamina,' said Goffanon seriously.

Two hours later and they were well ahead of the Fhoi Myore force. They sat in a dip in the ground, enjoying the smell of grass and wild flowers, knowing miserably that it would not be long before these became rigid with cold and died. Perhaps that was why Corum relished the smell of the vegetation while it was still there.

Goffanon let out a great sigh as, tenderly, without picking the plant, he looked at a wild poppy.

'The Mabden lands are amongst the prettiest in this whole Realm,' he said. 'And now these perish, as all the other lands have perished. Conquered by the Fhoi Myore.'

'What of the other lands in this Realm?' Corum asked. 'What know you of them?'

'Long-since turned to poisoned ice by the diseased remnants of the Fhoi Myore race,' Goffanon said. 'These lands were safe partly because the Fhoi Myore remembered Craig Dôn and avoided the place, partly because this is where the surviving Sidhi made their homes. It took them a considerable length of time before they came back from the eastern seas and beyond.' He stood up. 'Would you sit upon my shoulders now? It will be more comfortable for you I think.'

And Corum accepted the offer with courtesy and climbed upon the dwarf's shoulders. Then they were off again, for there was no time to be wasted.

'This proves the need for Mabden unity,' said Corum from his perch. 'If there were proper communications between the surviving Mabden, then all could gather to attack the Fhoi Myore force from several sides.'

'But what of Balahr and the rest? What have the Mabden in

their armouries which can defend against Balahr's frightful gaze?'

'They have their Treasures. Already I have seen how one of them, the spear Bryionak which you gave me, can do much harm to the Fhoi Myore.'

'There was only one spear Bryionak,' said Goffanon in an almost melancholy tone, 'and now that has vanished – doubtless returning to my own home realm.'

They entered a narrow gorge between white limestone cliffs topped by green turf.

'As I recall,' said Goffanon, 'the city of Caer Garanhir lies but a short way on the other side of the pass.'

But as the pass wound up through the rocks and grew narrower at its farther end, they saw that a group of figures awaited them there.

At first Corum thought that these were war-knights of the Tuha-na-Gwyddneu Garanhir, alerted of their coming and there to greet them. But then he noticed the greenish caste of riders and horses and he knew that these were not friends. And then the green ranks broke and another rider emerged – a rider whose armour shifted colour constantly and whose face was completely hidden by a blank, smooth helm.

And Goffanon stopped and took Corum from his shoulders and put him upon the pale clay of the ground and looked back as he heard a sound. Corum looked also.

Riding green horses down the steep slopes of the gorge came another group of green riders and the whole air was thick with their piny scent. The riders reached the bottom of the pass and paused.

Gaynor's voice echoed through the narrow walls of the gorge and his voice was gay, triumphant:

'You could have prolonged your life so easily, Prince Corum, if you had chosen to remain as my guest at Craig Dôn. Where is the little lamb Amergin, whom you stole?'

'Amergin was dying, the last I saw of him,' said Corum truthfully, unslinging his axe from his back.

Goffanon murmured: 'It is time for the hewing of pines, I think, Corum,' and he moved so that he stood facing those at their rear while Corum confronted those at their front. Goffanon hefted his own huge axe, turning its polished iron so that it flashed in the bright summer sunshine. 'At least we shall die in the summer warmth,' Goffanon said, 'and not have our bones eaten by the Cold Folk's mist.'

'You should have been warned,' said Prince Gaynor the Damned. 'He eats a diet of rare grasses only. And now the High King of the Mabden is perished, a mere carcass of mutton. No matter.'

In the distance, behind him, Corum heard a great roaring noise and he knew that this must be the Fhoi Myore on the march, moving much faster than he had thought possible.

Goffanon cocked his head on one side and listened almost curiously.

Then, from both sides, the green-faced horsemen began to bear down on them so that the sides of the gorge shook and Gaynor's bleak laughter grew wilder and wilder.

Corum whirled his war-axe and made a great wound in the neck of the first horse, seeing greenish, viscous liquid ooze from the gash. It halted the horse's momentum, but it did not kill it. Its green eyes rolled and its green teeth snapped and its green rider brought a dull iron sword down at Corum's head. Corum had fought Hew Argech, one of the People of the Pines, and he knew how to counter such blows. He chopped deliberately at the wrist as it swept down and wrist and sword flew earthward like a bough lopped from a tree. He chopped next at the horse's legs so that it crashed on to the dusty clay and lay there unsuccessfully trying to regain an upright position. This helped to confuse the next rider who came at Corum and was unable to strike a clean blow without snaring his horse's legs in those of the wounded animal. The scent of pines was now almost overpowering as the sap oozed from the wounds Corum wrought. It was a scent he had once loved but which now sickened him. It was sweet and it was odious.

Goffanon had brought at least three of the Pine Folk down and was chopping at their bodies, slicing off limbs so that they could not move, though they still lived, their green eyes glaring, their green lips snarling. These had once been the flower of Mabden warriors, probably from Caer Llud itself, but their human blood had been drawn from their veins and the pine sap poured into them instead, and now they served the Fhoi Myore for they were ashamed of what they had become and at the same time most proud of their distinction.

As he fought, Corum tried to glance about him to see if there was any means of escaping from the gorge, but Gaynor had chosen the best place to attack – where the sides were steepest and the passage narrowest. This meant that Corum and Goffanon could defend themselves longer but could never hope to get away. Eventually they would be overwhelmed by the People of the Pines, vanquished by these living trees, these brothers of the oak's oldest enemy. Like a rustling, marching forest, they rushed again at the one-eyed Vadhagh with the silver hand, at the eight-foot Sidhi with the bristling black beard.

And Gaynor, at a safe distance, laughed on. He was indulging in his favourite sport – the destruction of heroes, the conquest of honour, the extermination of virtue and idealism. And he indulged himself thus because he had never quite succeeded in driving these qualities from his own self.

Thus Gaynor sought to still any voice which dared remind him of the hope he dared not hope, the ambition he feared to entertain – the possibility of his own salvation.

Corum's arms grew weary and he staggered now as he chopped at the green arms, slashed at green heads, cracked the skulls of green horses and grew dizzy with the scent of the pine sap which was now sticky underfoot.

'Farewell, Goffanon,' he shouted to his comrade. 'It heartened me much when you joined our cause, but I fear your decision has led you to your death.'

And Corum was astonished when he heard Goffanon's laughter blending with that of Prince Gaynor the Damned.

7. A LONG-LOST
BROTHER

Then Corum realized that only Goffanon laughed.

Gaynor laughed no longer.

Corum tried to peer through the mass of green warriors to the far end of the pass where he had last seen Gaynor, but there was no sign of the flickering, fiery armour. It seemed that Prince Gaynor the Damned had deserted the scene of his triumph.

And now the Warriors of the Pines were falling back, looking fearfully into the sky. And Corum risked glancing up and he saw a rider there. The rider was seated upon a shining black horse all dressed in red and gilded leather, the buckles of its harness of sea-ivory and the edges all stitched with large and perfect pearls.

And overwhelming the stink of the pines came the fresh, warm smell of the sea. And Corum knew that the smell came from the smiling rider who sat the horse with one hand upon his hip and the other upon his bridle.

And then, casually, the rider stepped his horse over the gorge and turned so that he could look down into the pass from the other side. It gave Corum some idea of the size of horse and rider.

The rider had a light, golden beard and his face was that of a youth of some eighteen summers. His golden hair was braided and hung down his chest. He wore a breastplate which was fashioned from some kind of bronze and decorated with motifs of the the sun and of ships, as well as whales and fish and sea-serpents. Upon the rider's great, fair-skinned arms were bands of gold whose patterns matched those on the breastplate. He wore a blue cloak with a great circular pin at the left shoulder. His eyes were a clear piercing green-grey. At his hip was a heavy sword which was probably longer than Corum's full height. On his left arm was a shield of the same glowing bronze as his breastplate.

And Goffanon was crying delightedly up to the gigantic rider on the gigantic horse, even as he continued to fight the People of the Pines.

'I heard you coming, brother!' cried Goffanon. 'I heard you and knew who it was!'

And the giant's laughter rumbled down the gorge. 'Greetings, little Goffanon. You fight well. You always fought well.'

'Do you come to aid us?'

'It seems so. My rest was disturbed by the Fhoi Myore vermin laying ice across my ocean. For years I have been at peace in my underwater retreat, thinking to have no more irritation from the Cold Folk. But they came, with their ice and their mist and their silly soldiers, and so I must attempt to teach them a lesson.'

Almost carelessly he drew his great sword from its scabbard and with the flat reached down into the gorge to sweep away the Brothers of the Pines so that they began to retreat in panic in both directions.

'I will meet you at the far end of this pass,' said the giant, shaking the reins of his horse and making it move away from the brink. 'I fear I would stick if I tried to join you there.'

The ground shook as the gigantic rider disappeared and a little while later they trudged up to the end of the gorge to meet him and Goffanon in spite of his weariness ran forward with his arms wide open, the axe falling from his grip, shouting joyfully:

'Ilbrec! Ilbrec! Son of my old friend! I did not know you lived!'

Ilbrec, twice Goffanon's height, swung himself from his saddle, laughing.

'Aha, little smith, if I had known that you survived I should long since have sought you out!'

Corum was astonished to see the Sidhi, Goffanon, seized in

Ilbrec's great arms and embraced. Then Ilbrec turned his attention upon Corum and said:

'Smaller and smaller, eh! Who is this who so resembles our ancient Vadhagh cousins?'

'Vadhagh he is, brother Ilbrec. A champion of the Mabden since the Sidhi left.'

Corum felt ridiculously tiny as he bowed to the great, laughing youth. 'Greetings to you, cousin,' he said.

'And how fared your father, the great Manannan?' Goffanon asked. 'I heard that he had been slain in the Island of the West and lies now beneath his own Hill.'

'Aye – with a Mabden folk named for him. He has honour in this Realm.'

'And deservedly, Ilbrec.'

'Are there more of our folk surviving?' Ilbrec asked. 'I had thought myself the last.'

'None to my knowledge,' Goffanon told him.

'And how many Fhoi Myore are there?'

'Six. There were seven, but the Black Bull of Crinannass took one before it departed this Realm – or died – I know not which. The Black Bull was the last of the great Sidhi herd.'

'Six.' Ilbrec sat himself down upon the turf, his golden brow darkening. 'What are their names, these six?'

'One is Kerenos,' said Corum. 'Another is Balahr and another is Goim. The others I do not know.'

'Neither have I seen them,' said Goffanon. 'They hide, as usual, in their mist.'

Ilbrec nodded. 'Kerenos with his dogs, Balahr with his eye and Goim – Goim with her teeth. An unsavoury trio, eh? And hard to fight, those three alone. They were three of the most powerful. Doubtless it is why they linger on. I should have thought them all rotted and forgotten by now. They have vitality, these Fhoi Myore.'

'The vitality of Chaos and Old Night,' agreed Goffanon, fingering the blade of his axe. 'Ah, if only all our comrades were with us. What a reaving then, eh? And if those comrades wielded the Weapons of Light, how we should drive back the coldness and the darkness . . .'

'But we are two,' said Ilbrec sadly. 'And the greatest of the Sidhi are no more.'

'Yet the Mabden are courageous,' said Corum. 'They have a certain power. And if their High King can be restored to them . . .'

'True,' said Goffanon, and he began to tell his old friend of all that had passed in recent months, since the coming of the Fhoi Myore to the islands of the Mabden. Only when he spoke of Calatin and the wizard's charm did he become reticent, but managed to speak of the matter nonetheless.

'So the Golden Oak and the Silvern Ram still exist,' mused Ilbrec. 'My father spoke of them. And Fand the Beautiful, she prophesied that one day they would give power to the Mabden. My mother Fand was a great seeress, for all she had weaknesses in other directions.' Ilbrec grinned and spoke no more of Fand. Instead, he rose up and went to where his black horse cropped the grass. 'Now, I suppose, we must make speed for Caer Garanhir and see what defences they can build and how best we can help them when the Fhoi Myore attack. Do you think all six ride against that city?'

'It is possible,' said Corum. 'Yet usually the Fhoi Myore do not move in the front of their vassals but bring up the rear. They are cunning, in some ways, those Fhoi Myore.'

'They were ever that. Would you ride with me, Vadhagh?'

Corum smiled. 'If your horse agrees that he will not mistake me for a flea upon his back, I'll ride with you, Ilbrec.'

And, laughing, Ilbrec swung Corum up and sat him down so that he could place a leg either side of his great pearl-studded pommel. Still unused to the hugeness of the Sidhi (and understanding at last how Goffanon could regard himself as a dwarf), Corum felt weak in the presence of Ilbrec who now seated himself with a creak of leather breeks and saddle behind him, calling out:

'Onward, Splendid Mane. Onward, beautiful horse, to where the Mabden gather.'

And as soon as he had become used to the huge movements of the cantering horse, Corum began to enjoy the sensation of riding the beast, listening to the conversation of the two Sidhi as Goffanon continued his steady pace beside the horse.

'It seems to me,' said Ilbrec thoughtfully, 'that my father bequeathed a chest to me containing some armour and a spear or two. Perhaps they would be useful in this struggle of ours, though they have lain unused for many scores of years now. If I could find that chest I would know.'

'Yellow Shaft and Red Javelin?' Goffanon asked eagerly. 'The sword your father named Retaliator?'

'Most of his arms were lost in the last battle, as you know,' said Ilbrec. 'And others were of a sort which drew their strength from our original Realm and thus could not be used properly or could only be used once. Nonetheless, there could be something of use in that chest. It is one of the sea-caverns I have not visited since that battle. For all I know it has gone, or rotted, or,' he smiled, 'been devoured by some sea-monster.'

'Well, we shall know soon enough,' said Goffanon. 'And if Retaliator should be there ...'

'We'd be best advised to consider our own abilities,' said Ilbrec, laughing again. 'Rather than put our faith in weapons which might not even exist in this Realm any longer. Even with them, the strength of the Fhoi Myore is greater than ours.'

'But added to the Mabden strength,' said Corum, 'it could be great indeed.'

'I have always liked the Mabden,' Ilbrec told him, 'though I am not sure I share your faith in its powers. Still, times change and so do races. I will give you my judgement of the Mabden when I have seen them do battle against the Fhoi Myore.'

'That opportunity should come quite soon,' said Corum, pointing ahead.

He had seen the towers of Caer Garanhir. And they were tall, those towers, rivalling the buildings of Caer Llud in size and outshining them in beauty. Towers of shining limestone and dark-veined obsidian from which banners flew. Towers surrounded by the battlements of a massive wall which spoke of invincible strength.

Yet Corum knew that the impression of strength was deceptive, that Balahr's horrid eye could crack that granite and destroy all who sheltered behind it. Even with the giant Ilbrec as an ally they would be hard put to resist the forces of the Fhoi Myore.

8. THE GREAT FIGHT
AT CAER GARANHIR

Corum had smiled when he saw the expressions of those who had come to the battlements when Ilbrec had shouted, but now his face was dark as he stood in King Daffyn's magnificent hall, all hung with jewelled flags, and tried to speak to a man who was barely able to stand and yet continued to sip from a mead-cup as he tried to listen to Corum's words.

Half of King Daffyn's war-knights were sprawled insensible beside benches covered with stained samite. The other half leaned on anything which would give them support, some with drawn swords calling out silly boasts, while some sat with mouths hanging open, staring at Ilbrec who had managed to squeeze himself into the hall and crouched behind Corum and Goffanon.

They were not prepared for war, the Tuha-na-Gwyddneu Garanhir. They were prepared for nothing but drunken slumber now, for they had been celebrating a marriage – the marriage of the king's son, Prince Guwinn, to the daughter of a great knight of Caer Garanhir.

Those still awake were impressed well enough by the appearance of what they saw as three Sidhi of varying size, but some were still certain that they suffered the effects of feasting and drinking too much.

'The Fhoi Myore march in strength against you, King Daffyn,' said Corum again. 'Many hundreds of warriors and most hard to slay, they are!'

King Daffyn's face was red with drink. He was a fat, intelligent-looking man, but his eyes held little intelligence at that moment.

'I fear you overpraised the Mabden, Prince Corum,' said Ilbrec tolerantly. 'We must do what we can without them.'

'Wait!' King Daffyn came unsteadily down the steps from his throne, mead-horn still in his hand. 'Are we to be slain in our cups?'

'It seems so, King Daffyn,' said Corum.

'Drunk? Slain without dignity by those who slew – who slew our brothers of the East?'

'Just so!' said Goffanon, turning away impatiently. 'And you deserve little better.'

King Daffyn fingered the great medallion of rank which he wore about his neck. 'I shall have failed my people,' he said.

'Listen again,' said Corum. And he re-told his tale, slowly, while King Daffyn made a considerable effort to understand, even throwing away the mead-horn and refusing more mead when a blustering knight offered it to him.

'How many hours are they from Caer Garanhir?' asked the king when Corum had finished.

'Perhaps three. We travelled rapidly. Perhaps four or five. Perhaps they will not attack at all until the morning.'

'But three hours – we have three hours for certain.'

'I think so.'

King Daffyn staggered about his hall, shaking sleeping knights, shouting at those who were still in some stage of wakefulness. And Corum despaired.

Ilbrec voiced that despair. 'This will not do at all,' he said. He began to squeeze himself back through the doors. 'Not at all.'

Corum barely heard him as he continued to remonstrate with King Daffyn who was fighting with his own disinclination to hear bad news on such a day as this.

Goffanon turned and left the hall shouting. 'Do not abandon them, Ilbrec. You see them at their worst . . . '

But there came a shaking of the earth, a thundering of hooves, and Corum now ran from the hall in time to see the huge black horse, Splendid Mane, leap the battlements of Caer Garanhir's walls.

'So,' said Corum, 'he has gone. Plainly he feels he would best save his strength for a better cause. I cannot say that I blame him.'

'He is headstrong,' said Goffanon. 'Like his father. But his father would not have left friends behind.'

'You wish to go, too?'

'No. I'll stay. I've told you my decision. We are lucky to be here and not fallen to the Pine Folk. We should be grateful that Ilbrec saved our lives once.'

'Aye.' Wearily, Corum turned back into the hall to find King Daffyn shaking two of the prone warriors.

'Wake up!' said King Daffyn. 'Wake up. The Fhoi Myore come!'

They stood blinking upon the battlements, their eyes red, their hands shaking, and they made much use of the water-skins which the young lads brought round. Some were still in their formal wedding finery and others had donned armour. Now they sighed and groaned and held their heads as they looked out from the walls of Caer Garanhir and waited for the enemy.

'Yonder!' said a boy to Corum, lowering his water-skin and pointing. 'I see a cloud!'

Corum looked and he saw it. A cloud of boiling mist on the far horizon.

'Aye,' he said. 'That is the Fhoi Myore. But many come ahead of them, look. Look lower. See the riders.'

It seemed for a moment that a green tidal wave washed towards Caer Garanhir.

'What is that, Prince Corum?' said the boy.

'It is the People of the Pines,' said Corum, 'and they are exceptionally hard to slay.'

'The mist moved towards us, but now it has paused,' said the boy.

'Aye,' Corum replied, 'that is how the Fhoi Myore always fight, sending their vassals to weaken us first.'

He looked along the battlements. One of King Daffyn's war-knights was leaning out and groaning as he vomited. Corum turned away in grim despair. Other warriors were coming up the stone stairways now, nocking arrows to long bows. These, it appeared, had not celebrated the marriage of Prince Guwinn with quite the same abandon as the knights. They wore shining shirts of bronze mail and there were bronze war-caps upon their dark red heads. Some wore leathern breeks, and others had mail leggings. As well as the quivers on their backs they had javelins and there were swords or axes at their belts. Corum's spirits lifted a little as he saw these soldiers, but they dropped again when he heard, from the far distance, the cold, booming, wordless voices of the Fhoi Myore. No matter how bravely or how well they fought this day, the Fhoi Myore remained and the Fhoi Myore had the means of destroying all within Caer Garanhir's splendid walls.

Now the sound of hooves drowned the voices of the Fhoi Myore. Pale green horses and pale green riders, all of the same shade, with pale green clothing and pale green swords in pale green hands. The riders spread out as they approached the walls, circling to find the weakest parts of the defences before they closed in.

And the sweet, nauseating smell of the pines drifted closer on the wind and that same wind brought a chill which made all who stood upon the battlements shiver.

'Archers!' King Daffyn cried, raising his long sword high. 'Let fly!'

And a wave of whirring arrows met the wave of green riders and had no more effect upon them than if the archers had shot their shafts into so many trees. Faces, bodies, limbs were struck, horses were struck, and the People of the Pines did not waver.

A young knight in a long samite robe, over which had hastily been thrown a mail surcoat, ran up the steps, buckling a sword about his waist. He was a handsome youth, his brown hair unbound, his dark eyes dazed and puzzled. His feet were bare, Corum noticed.

'Father!' the youth cried, approaching King Daffyn. 'I am here!' And this must be Prince Guwinn, less drunk than his fellows. And Corum thought to himself that Prince Guwinn had most to lose this day, for he must have come straight from his marriage bed.

Now Corum saw fire flickering in the distance and knew that Gaynor came to war. At the head of his Ghoolegh infantry, Gaynor the Damned lifted up his faceless helm as if he sought Corum amongst the defenders, his yellow plume dancing and his naked sword glowing sometimes silver, sometimes scarlet, sometimes gold and sometimes blue, the eight-arrowed Sign of Chaos pulsing on his breastplate, his strange armour glowing with as many different colours as his sword. Gaynor's tall horse pranced before the white-faced Ghooleg infantry. Corum saw red, bestial eyes gleaming in a thousand faces. And yet still there seemed to be more fire, fire burning on the fringes of the Fhoi Myore mist. Was this some new form of enemy Corum had not yet encountered?

The People of the Pines were driving closer and from their mouths came laughter – rustling laughter like the sound of wind through leaves. Corum had heard such laughter before and he feared it.

He saw the reaction in the faces of the knights and warriors who waited on the battlements. They all felt terror strike them as they realized fully that they faced the supernatural. Then each man controlled his terror as best he could and prepared to stand against the Brothers to the Trees.

Another wave of arrows flew out, and another, and every single arrow found its target and now virtually every pine warrior rode forward with a red-fletched arrow protruding from his heart.

And the rustling laughter increased.

The warriors rode slowly and relentlessly forward. Some bristled with arrows. A few had javelins sticking completely through them. But their blank faces grinned blank grins and their cold eyes remained fixed upon the defenders. Reaching the foot of the walls, they dismounted.

More arrows flew and some of the People of the Pines began to take on the appearance of strange, sharp-spined animals, so many arrows quivered in their bodies.

And then they began to climb the walls.

They climbed as if they needed no hand- or foot-holds at all. They climbed as ivy climbed. Green tendrils moving up the walls towards the defenders.

One or two of the knights gasped and fell back, unable to accept this sight. Corum hardly blamed them. Nearby Goffanon growled in distaste.

And the first of the pale green warriors, eyes still fixed, grins still rigid, reached the battlements and began to attempt to climb over.

Corum's war-axe flashed in the sunlight and its blade smashed the head completely from the first warrior he saw. That warrior he pushed backward and it fell, but immediately another appeared and Corum's axe again struck off the head. Green sap spouted from the neck and clung to the blade of the axe, spattered across the stones of the battlements as he drew back his arms to strike again at the next head. He knew that he must tire of this soon or that parts of the defences would weaken and he would be attacked from both sides, but he did what he could while the People of the Pines swarmed up the walls, apparently in inexhaustible numbers.

There came a momentary pause when Corum was able to look beyond the Pine Warriors and see Gaynor ordering his Ghoolegh forward. They carried great logs in leathern harness which swung between them and they were plainly intent on battering down the gates of the city. Knowing that the Mabden were not, these days, used to fighting sieges, Corum could think of no way to resist the battering rams. The Mabden had fought hand to hand for centuries, each man picking another from the ranks of his enemies. Many tribes had not even fought to kill, feeling it ignoble to slay a man when he had been defeated. And while this was a Mabden strength it was, in any fight with Fhoi Myore forces, a great weakness.

Corum yelled to King Daffyn to prepare his people for the appearance of the Ghoolegh in their streets, but King Daffyn was kneeling, his face gleaming with tears, and a Pine Warrior was running along the battlements towards Corum.

Corum saw that King Daffyn knelt beside the body of one whom the Pine Warrior had just slain. The body was dressed in white samite and a mail coat. Prince Guwinn would not be returning to his marriage bed.

Corum swung the axe low and chopped the Pine Warrior at the waist so that the torso toppled from the legs as a tree might topple. For moments the warrior continued to live, the legs moving forward, the arms waving from where the torso lay upon the flagstones. Then it died and turned brown almost immediately.

Corum ran up to King Daffyn crying savagely:

'Do not weep for your son – avenge him! Fight on, King Daffyn, or you and your folk are surely lost.'

'Fight on? Why? What I lived for has died. And we shall all die soon, Prince Corum. Why not now? I care not how I perish.'

'For love,' said Corum, 'and for beauty. For those things must you fight. For courage and pride!' But even as he spoke such words they rang hollow as he looked upon the corpse of the youth and he saw the tears spring away into the eyes of the youth's father. He turned away.

From below came the crashing and creaking noises as the battering rams repeatedly struck the gates. On the battlements Pine Warriors were now almost as thick as the defenders.

Goffanon could be seen, his huge bulk rising above a mass of the People of the Pines, his double-bladed axe swinging with the regularity of a pendulum as it chopped and chopped at the tree folk. There seemed to be a song on Goffanon's lips, almost a dirge, as he fought, and Corum caught some of the words.

> *I have been in the place where was slain Gwendoleu,*
> *The son of Ceidaw, the pillar of songs,*
> *When ravens screamed over blood.*

> *I have been in the place where Bran was killed,*
> *The son of Iweridd, of far extending fame,*
> *When the ravens of the battlefield screamed.*

> *I have been where Llacheu was slain,*
> *The son of Urtu, extolled in songs,*
> *When the ravens screamed over blood.*

> *I have been where Meurig was killed,*
> *The son of Carreian, of honourable fame,*
> *When the ravens screamed over flesh.*

> *I have been where Gwallawg was killed,*
> *The son of Goholeth, the accomplished,*
> *The resister of Lloegyr, the son of Lleynawg.*

> *I have been where the soldiers of the Mabden were slain,*
> *From the east to the north:*
> *I am the escort of the grave.*

> *I have been where the soldiers of the Mabden were slain,*
> *From the east to the south:*
> *I am alive, they in death!*

And Corum realized that this was Goffanon's death-song, that the Sidhi smith prepared himself for his own inevitable slaying.

> *I have been to the graves of the Sidhi,*
> *From the east to the west:*
> *Now the ravens scream for me!*

9. THE DEFENCE OF
THE KING'S HALL

Corum realized that the position upon the battlements was all but lost and he smashed through the Pine Warriors to stand beside Goffanon, crying:

'To the hall, Goffanon! Fall back to the hall!'

Goffanon's song ended and he looked at Corum with calm eyes.

'Very well,' he said.

Together they went slowly back to the steps, fighting all the way, the People of the Pines crowding in on all sides, fixed grins, fixed eyes, sword-arms rising and falling. And the rustling, terrifying laughter hissing forever from their lips.

The knights and warriors who survived followed Corum's example and barely made the street as the timbers of the gates burst and the brass-shod battering ram smashed through. Two knights escorted King Daffyn who was still weeping and at length they reached the king's hall and drew the great brass doors close, barring them.

The signs of festivity were still everywhere about the hall. There were even a few too drunk to be roused who would probably die without realizing what had happened. Brands guttered, jewelled flags drooped. Corum went to peer through the narrow windows and saw that Gaynor was there, riding triumphantly at the head of his half-dead army, the eight-arrowed Sign of Chaos glowing as radiantly as ever upon his chest. For a while at least, Corum hoped, the people of the city would be reasonably safe while Gayner concentrated his attack upon the hall. Corum saw the Ghoolegh behind Gaynor. They still carried their battering rams. And still the Fhoi Myore had not moved forward. Corum wondered if they would advance at all, knowing that Gaynor, the Ghoolegh and the People of the Pines could accomplish the defeat of Caer Garanhir without their help.

Yet even if, by hard fighting, the Fhoi Myore vassals could be vanquished, Corum knew that the Fhoi Myore could not be.

Pale green faces began to appear at the windows and stained glass smashed as the People of the Pines attempted to gain entrance to the hall. Again the knights and warriors of the Tuha-na-Gwyddneu Garanhir ran to defend themselves against the inhuman invaders.

Swords of notched and shining iron met the pale green swords of the Pine Warriors and the fight continued while outside the steady pounding of the battering rams began to sound on the bronze doors of the hall.

And while the fight raged, King Daffyn sat upon his throne, his head upon his hands, and wept for the death of Prince Guwinn, taking no interest in how the battle progressed.

Corum ran to where at least ten of the Pine Warriors bore down on two of King Daffyn's war-knights. His axe was blunted now and his fleshly hand was sore and bleeding. If it had not been for his silver hand, he might long since have been forced to drop the weapon. As it was, his arms were weary as he lifted the double-bladed axe to chop at the neck of a Pine Warrior who was about to slide his sword into the unprotected side of a tall knight already engaged with two more of the Pine Folk.

Several of the Pine Warriors came at Corum then, swords slashing, laughter rustling from their pale green lips, and Corum took first one step backward and then another as they pressed him towards the far wall of the hall. Elsewhere Goffanon was engaged with three of the warriors and unable to help Corum. The Vadhagh prince swung the axe back and forth, up and down, and swords ripped his byrnie and found his flesh and began to draw blood from a dozen shallow wounds.

Then Corum felt the stones of the wall behind him and knew he could retreat no further. Above him a brand flickered, casting his shadow over the bodies of the Pine Folk as, grinning, they moved to finish him.

A sword bit into the haft of his axe. Desperately he wrenched the weapon free and struck at the one who held the sword, a warrior who had been handsome but whose face was now pierced by three red-fletched arrows. He struck the axe deep into the skull, splitting it. Green gore spouted, the warrior fell but he took the head and part of the haft of Corum's axe with him. Corum turned and leapt for the ledge above his head, getting his balance and drawing his sword, steadying himself with his silver hand by clinging to the bracket in which the brand flared. The Pine Warriors began to move up the wall towards him. He kicked one back, chopped at another with his sword, but they were clutching at his feet now, still grinning, still laughing, cold eyes still staring. Desperately he released his grip upon the bracket and seized the brand, plunging it into the face of the nearest warrior.

And the warrior screamed.

For the first time a Pine Warrior yelled in pain. And his face began to burn, the sap sizzling from the wounds he had already received but which had not appeared to harm him.

The other warriors fell away in panic, avoiding their blazing comrade as he ran about the hall screaming and burning until at last he fell over the remains of another of his kind. The brown body caught, too, and began to burn.

And then Corum cursed himself for not understanding that the only weapon likely to be feared by tree-folk was fire. He called to the others:

'Get brands! Fire will destroy them! Take the torches from the walls!'

And he saw that the bronze doors of the hall were bulging now and could not last much longer before the onslaught of the Ghoolegh battering rams.

Now all who could still move were springing to the torches and tearing them down, turning them upon their enemies, and soon the hall was full of cloudy smoke – smoke which choked Corum and the others – sweet, pine-scented smoke.

The People of the Pines began to retreat, trying to reach the windows, but the war-knights of the Tuha-na-Gwyddneu Garanhir stopped them, thrusting the brands into their bodies and making them shriek and fall upon the bloody flagstones as they burned.

And then there fell a silence in the hall – a silence broken only by the steady beating of the rams upon the door. And there were no more People of the Pines, only grey ash and smoke and a sweet, nauseating stink.

Here and there the jewelled flags had caught and were beginning to smoulder. Elsewhere wooden beams were burning, but the defenders ignored them as they massed near the front of the hall and waited for the Ghoolegh to come.

And this time each surviving warrior, including Corum and the battered Sidhi smith Goffanon, had a brand in his hand.

The bronze door bulged. The hinges and the bars creaked.

Light began to show through as the doors were beaten out of shape.

Again the rams struck. Again the doors creaked.

Through the gap Corum thought he saw Gaynor directing the work of the Ghoolegh.

Another blow and one of the bars snapped and flew across the hall to land at the feet of the king who still wept in his throne at the far end.

Another blow and the second bar snapped and a hinge clattered to the flagstones, the door tilting and beginning to swing inward.

Another blow.

And the bronze doors fell and the Ghoolegh paused in surprise as a wedge of men came running towards them from the smoky gloom of the hall at Caer Garanhir, brands in their left hands, swords or axes in their right hands, moving to attack.

Gaynor's black horse reared and the Damned Prince almost dropped his glowing sword in astonishment as he saw the battle-weary, smoke-blackened, tattered force, led by the Vadhagh Corum and the Sidhi Goffanon, rushing at him. 'What? What? Some still alive?'

Corum ran straight for Gaynor, but still Gaynor refused to do combat with him, turning the rearing horse and seeking to cut a path through his own Ghoolegh half-dead so that he might escape.

'Come back, Gaynor! Fight me! Oh, fight me, Gaynor!' cried Corum.

But Gaynor laughed his bleak laugh as he retreated. 'I shall not return to Limbo – not while the prospect of death awaits me in this Realm.'

'You forget that the Fhoi Myore are already dying. What if you outlive them? What if they perish and the world is renewed?'

'That cannot happen, Corum. Their poisons spread and are permanent! You fight for nothing, you see!'

Then Gaynor had gone and the Ghoolegh with their cutlasses

and their knives were lumbering forward, nervous of the brand-fire, for fire had no place in the Fhoi Myore lands. Though the Ghoolegh did not burn as the People of the Pines had burned, they feared the flames heartily and were loath to move forward, particularly now that Gaynor had retreated and could be seen in the distance turning his horse to watch the fray from safety.

The Ghoolegh outnumbered the survivors of Garanhir by more than ten to one, yet the war-knights and the warriors were forcing them backward, yelling their battle-cries, shouting their battle-songs, hacking and stabbing at the half-dead warriors, shoving the brands deep into their faces so that they grumbled and whined and put up their hands to ward away the flames.

And Goffanon was no longer singing his own death-song. He was laughing and shouting out to Corum: 'They retreat! They retreat! See how they retreat, Corum!'

But Corum felt no gaiety, for he knew that the Fhoi Myore had not yet attacked.

Then he heard Gaynor's voice calling:

'Balahr! Kerenos! Goim!' Gaynor called. 'It is time! It is time!'

Gaynor the Damned rode back to the gates of Caer Garanhir.

'Arek! Bress! Sreng! It is time! It is time!'

And Gaynor went shouting through the ruined gates of Caer Garanhir, his Ghoolegh fleeing behind him, thinking that he retreated.

Corum and Goffanon and the few knights and warriors of the Tuha-na-Gwyddneu Garanhir roared their triumph as they saw their enemies flee.

'For all that it shall be our only victory this day,' said Corum to Goffanon, 'I savour it greatly, my Sidhi friend.'

And then they waited for the Fhoi Myore to come.

But the Fhoi Myore did not come, though it began to grow dark. In the distance the Fhoi Myore mist remained and a few Ghoolegh milled here and there, mixing with the People of the Pines, but the Fhoi Myore, unused to defeat, were perhaps debating what to do next. Perhaps they recalled the Spear Bryionak and the Black Bull of Crinanass which had defeated them once, slaying their comrade, and seeing their vassals driven back, became fearful that another Bull came against them. Just as they avoided Craig Dôn it was possible that they now avoided Caer Mahlod because they associated it with defeat and were considering avoiding Caer Garanhir for the same reason.

Whatever made the Fhoi Myore remain upon the horizon Corum did not care. He was glad for the reprieve and the time for the dead to be counted, the wounded tended, the old and the children to be taken to places of greater security, the warriors and knights (many of whom were women) to be properly equipped and for the gates to be shored up as well as possible.

'They are cautious, the Fhoi Myore,' said Goffanon reminiscently. 'They are like cowardly carrion dogs. It is what has allowed them to survive so long, I think.'

'And Gaynor follows their example. As far as I know he has no great reason to fear me, but it worked to our advantage this day. Yet the Fhoi Myore will come soon, I think,' said Corum.

'I think so,' agreed the Sidhi. He stood on the battlements beside Corum and sharpened the blades of his axe with the whetstone he carried, his great, black brows drawn together. 'Yet do you see something which flickers close to the mist? And do you see a darker mist blending with that of the Fhoi Myore?'

'I saw it earlier,' Corum said, 'and cannot explain it. I think it is some other Fhoi Myore tool which they shall send against us before long.'

'Ah,' said Goffanon pointing. 'Here comes Ilbrec. Doubtless he saw that our battle went well and comes to join us again.' Goffanon's tone was bitter.

They watched the gigantic, golden youth riding the proud black stallion towards them. Ilbrec was smiling and he carried a sword in his hand. The sword was not that which he still bore at his belt, but another. And it made the sword he bore at his belt seem crude and poor by comparison, for it blazed as brightly as the sun and its hilt was all worked in fine gold and there were jewels in it and a pommel which glowed like a ruby and yet was the size of Corum's head. Ilbrec tossed his braids and waved the sword high.

'You were right to remind me of the Weapons of Light, Goffanon! I found the chest and I found the sword. Here it is! Here is Retaliator, my father's sword with which he fought the Fhoi Myore. Here is Retaliator!'

And Goffanon said sullenly, as Ilbrec came closer to the walls, his huge head level with theirs as they stood upon the battlements: 'But you came with it too late, Ilbrec. We have finished our fight now.'

'Too late? Did I not use the sword to draw a circle around the Fhoi Myore ranks so that even now they are confused, unable to move towards the city, unable to direct their troops?'

'So it was your work!' Corum began to laugh. 'You saved us, after all, Ilbrec, when you seemed to have deserted us?'

Ilbrec was puzzled. 'Desert you? I? Leave what will be the last struggle between Sidhi and Fhoi Myore ever to take place? I would not do that, little Vadhagh!'

And Goffanon was laughing now.

'I know you would not, Ilbrec. Welcome back to us! And welcome, too, to the great sword Retaliator!'

'It still has all its powers,' said Ilbrec, turning the blade to make it blaze yet more brightly. 'It is still the mightiest weapon ever drawn against the Fhoi Myore. And they know it! Ah, they know it, Goffanon! I drew this burning circle around their poison mist, containing the mist and containing them at the same time, for they cannot move unless their mist moves with them. And there they stay.'

'For ever?' Corum said hopefully.

Ilbrec shook his head and smiled. 'No. Not for ever, but for a while. And before we leave I will draw a defence about Caer Garanhir so that the Fhoi Myore and their warriors will fear to attack.'

'We must go to King Daffyn and interrupt his grieving, I fear,' said Corum. 'Time grows short if we are to save Amergin's life. We need the Golden Oak and the Silvern Ram.'

King Daffyn raised his red eyes and looked upon Corum and Goffanon who stood in the hall before him. A slender girl of little more than sixteen summers sat upon the arm of the king's chair and stroked the king's head.

'Your city is safe now, King Daffyn, and will be so for some time. But now we ask a boon of you!'

'Go,' said King Daffyn. 'I suppose that I shall be grateful to you later, but I am not grateful now. Please leave me. Sidhi warriors bring the Fhoi Myore upon us.'

'The Fhoi Myore marched before we came here,' said Corum. 'It was our warning that saved you.'

'It did not save my son,' said King Daffyn.

'It did not save my husband,' said the maiden who sat beside the king.

'But other sons were saved – and other husbands – and more will be saved, King Daffyn, with your help. We seek two of the Mabden Treasures – the Oak of Gold and the Ram of Silver. Do you have them?'

'They are no longer mine,' said King Daffyn. 'And I would not part with them if they were.'

'These are the only things which will revive your Archdruid Amergin from the enchantment put upon him by the Fhoi Myore,' said Corum.

'Amergin? He is a prisoner in Caer Llud. Or dead, by now.'

'No. Amergin lives – just. We saved him.'

'Did you – ' King Daffyn looked at the two with a different expression in his eyes. 'Amergin lives and is free?' The despair seemed to fall away as Fhoi Myore snow had melted when touched by the Black Bull's blood. 'Free? To guide us?'

'Aye – if we can get to Caer Mahlod in time. For that is where he is. At Caer Mahlod, but dying. The Oak and the Ram alone will save him. Yet if they are not yours, whom must we ask to give them to us?'

'They were our wedding gifts,' said the sweet-faced girl. 'They were the king's gifts to his son and me this morning, when Guwinn lived. You may have the Oak of Gold and the Ram of Silver.'

And she left the hall and returned shortly bearing a casket. And she opened the casket and revealed a model of a spreading oak tree all worked in gold and so fine as to seem completely real. And beside it rested the silver image of a ram, each curl of wool seeming to be shown by the craftsman who had made it. A ram with great, sweeping horns. A rampant ram whose silver eyes stared with a strange wisdom from the silver head.

And the maiden bowed her fair head and she closed the lid of the casket and she handed it to Corum who accepted it with gratitude, thanking her, thanking King Daffyn.

'And now we go back to Caer Mahlod,' said Corum.

'Tell Amergin, if he revives, that we shall follow him in any decision he cares to make,' said King Daffyn.

'I will tell him,' said Corum.

Then the Vadagh Prince and the Sidhi dwarf left that hall of mourning and went out through the gates of Caer Garanhir and joined their comrade Ibrec, son of Manannan, the greatest of the Sidhi heroes.

And the fire still flickered around the distant mist and now a

8

peculiar fire had begun to sprout some distance from the walls of Caer Garanhir.

'The Sidhi fire protects this place,' said Ilbrec. 'It will not last, but it will dissuade the Fhoi Myore from attacking, I think. Now, we ride!' He stuffed the sword Retaliator into his belt and bent to pick up Corum who clung to his casket as he was lifted into the air and sat upon Ilbrec's saddle near the pommel.

'We shall need a boat when we reach the sea,' said Corum as they began to move.

'Oh, I think not,' said Ilbrec.

Book Three

In which Prince Corum is witness
to the power of the Oak and the
Ram and the Mabden people
find new hope

1. THE ROAD ACROSS
THE WATER

They had reached the beach before Corum became aware that Goffanon was lagging behind. He craned his head back and saw that the Sidhi dwarf was some distance off, almost stumbling now and shaking his shaggy head from side to side.

'What ails Goffanon?' Corum said.

Ilbrec had not noticed. Now he, too, looked back. 'Perhaps he tires. He has fought long today and he has run many miles.' Ilbrec looked west, to where the sun was sinking. 'Should we rest before crossing the sea?'

The gigantic horse Splendid Mane tossed his head as if to say that he did not wish to rest, but Ilbrec laughed and patted his neck.

'Splendid Mane hates to rest and loves only to be galloping the world. He has slept for so long in the caverns beneath the sea that he is impatient to be on the move! But we must let Goffanon catch up with us and then ask him what he feels.'

Corum heard Goffanon's panting breath behind him and turned again, smiling, to ask the Sidhi smith what he wished to do.

But Goffanon's eyes were glaring and Goffanon's lips were curled back in a foam-flecked snarl and the great double-bladed war-axe was aimed directly at Ilbrec's skull.

'Ilbrec!' Corum flung himself towards the ground and landed

with a crash, managing to keep the chest containing the Oak and the Ram tucked firmly under his left arm. He drew his sword as he sprang upright, while Ilbrec turned, calling in puzzlement:

'Goffanon! Old friend? What's this?'

'He is enchanted!' Corum yelled. 'A Mabden wizard has put him under a glamour. Calatin must be nearby!'

Ilbrec reached out to grasp the haft of the dwarf's war-axe, but Goffanon was strong. He pulled the giant from his saddle and the two immortals began to struggle upon the ground, close to the sea-washed beach, while Corum and Splendid Mane looked on, the horse severely puzzled by his master's behaviour.

Corum cried: 'Goffanon! Goffanon! You fight a brother!'

Another voice floated down from above and looking up Corum saw a tall man standing on the edge of the cliff, a tendril or two of white, clinging mist drifting about his shoulders.

The world grew grey as the sun sank.

The figure on the cliff-edge was the wizard Calatin, in a long pleated surcoat of soft leather stained a rich, deep blue. Upon his slender, gloved fingers were jewelled rings and at his throat a collar of jewelled gold, while his samite robe was embroidered with mystical designs. He stroked his grey beard and he smiled his secret smile.

'He is my ally now, Corum of the Silver Hand,' said the wizard Calatin.

'And thus the ally of the Fhoi Myore!' Corum looked for a pathway up the cliff which would take him to the wizard and all the while Goffanon and Ilbrec tumbled over and over on the sand, grunting and snorting in their exertions.

'For the moment, at least,' said Calatin. 'But one does not have to be loyal to either Mabden or Fhoi Myore – or Sidhi – there are other loyalties, loyalties to oneself among them, are there not? And, who knows, but you could be an ally of mine soon!'

'Never that!' Corum began to run up a steep cliff path towards the wizard, his sword in his fleshly hand. 'Never that, Calatin!'

Out of breath, Corum reached the top of the cliff and approached the wizard, who smiled and began to retreat slowly.

It was then that Corum saw the mist behind the wizard and he recognized the mist for what it was.

'Fhoi Myore! One of them is free!'

'He was never trapped by Ilbrec's sword. We followed behind

112

the main force. This is Sreng. Sreng of the Seven Swords.'

And the mist began to move towards Corum as darkness covered the world and from below on the beach he still heard the pantings and the gruntings of the two fighting Sidhi.

And through the mist he saw a huge wicker battle-cart, large enough to take one as large as Ilbrec himself. The cart was drawn by two massive creatures which seemed most to resemble lizards, though they were not lizards. And from the cart now stepped a vast being with a white body all covered in red, pulsing warts, and the body was naked save for a belt. The belt was festooned with swords, making a sort of kilt. Corum looked up and he saw a face which was human in some respects and resembled the face of one he had known, long ago. The eyes were fierce and tragic. They were the eyes of the Earl of Krae, of Glandyth who had first struck off Corum's hand and put out his eye and so begun the long history of the fight against the Sword Rulers. But the eyes did not know Corum, though there was a flicker of recognition as they saw the silver hand fixed to his left wrist.

And from the torn folds of the mouth there sounded a booming noise.

'Lord Sreng,' said the wizard Calatin. 'This is he who helped in the destruction at Caer Mahlod. This is he who engineered this day's defeat. This is Corum.'

And Corum put down the casket in which reposed the Oak of Gold and the Ram of Silver and he spread his legs so that he stood firmly over the casket, and he reached to his belt and he took his dirk in his silver hand, and he prepared to defend himself against Sreng of the Seven Swords.

Sreng moved slowly, as if in pain, drawing two of his great swords from his belt.

'Slay Corum, Lord Sreng, and give me his body. Slay Corum and the Fhoi Myore will no longer be plagued by the resistance of the Mabden.'

Again the strained, booming noise came from the ragged mouth. The red warts pulsed on the vast expanse of pale flesh. Corum noted that one of the giant's legs was shorter than the other so that his gait was rolling as he moved. He saw that Sreng had only three teeth in his mouth and that the little finger of his right hand was covered in a yellow mould speckled with white and black. Then Corum saw that other parts of the giant's body, particularly about the thighs covered by the swords, also had patches of this mould growing upon them. And from Sreng

of the Seven Swords there escaped a foulness of stench remind-
ing Corum of long-dead fish and the excrement of cats.

From the dark below came the grunts of the fighting Sidhi.
Calatin was barely visible, chuckling from the night. Only
Sreng, framed against the mist he must carry always with him,
was clearly seen.

Corum felt that he did not wish to die at the hands of this
decrepit god, this Sreng. Sreng himself was already dying, as
were the other Fhoi Myore, of diseases which might take a
hundred years to kill him.

'Sreng,' said Corum, 'would you return to Limbo, return to
your Realm where you would not perish? I could help you go
back to your world, the plane where your disease will not
flourish. Leave this Realm to enjoy its natural state. Take back
your coldness and your death.'

'He deceives you, Lord Sreng,' said the wizard Calatin from
the darkness. 'Believe me. He deceives you.'

And then a word, a booming word escaped the torn lips. And
that word echoed the word Corum had spoken, as if it were the
only word in human speech which the lips could form.

The word was: 'Death.'

'Your own Realm awaits you – there is a way through.'

A diseased arm began to raise a crude sword of roughly
cast iron. Corum knew that he could not block any blow from
that sword. It whistled down at his head and then struck the
ground near his feet with horrible force. He realized that
Sreng had not deliberately missed him but that the Fhoi Myore
was hard put to control his limbs. Knowing this Corum stooped,
picked up the casket containing the Oak and the Ram, and ran
inside Sreng's guard, driving his sword deep into the giant's
shin.

The Fhoi Myore's voice boomed in pain. Corum ran under
his legs and hacked at him behind his knee where grew more of
the disgusting mildew. Sreng began to turn, but then the leg
buckled and he fell, searching for Corum while Calatin yelled:

'There, Lord Sreng! There! Behind you!'

Now Corum shuddered as the chilling mist began to eat at
his bones. All his instincts made him wish to run clear of the
mist and into the night, but he held his ground as a gigantic
hand came hunting for him. He hacked at the sinews of the
hand and then another huge sword whistled over his head
forcing him to duck, almost striking him.

And Sreng fell backward upon Corum, his neck pressing the

Vadhagh prince to the ground, his hand still searching for the mortal who fought him with such temerity.

Corum sweated to pull himself free, not knowing if any of his bones were broken, while the diseased fingers brushed his shoulder, sought to pluck him up, missed and began to search again. The stench of the Fhoi Myore's rotting flesh almost robbed Corum of his consciousness; the texture of that flesh made him shudder; the chilling mist robbed him of the last of his strength, but at least, he assured himself, he would have died valiantly against one of the great enemies of those whose cause he championed.

Was the voice he now heard Calatin's?

'Sreng! I know you, Sreng!'

No, the voice was Ilbrec's. So Ilbrec had won the fight and doubtless Goffanon now lay dead upon the beach. Corum had the impression of a huge hand coming down upon him, but then it seized Sreng by what was left of the Fhoi Myore's hair and pulled the head up so that Corum was able to scramble free. Then, as Corum staggered back, still keeping his hold upon the casket containing the Oak and the Ram, he saw golden Ilbrec draw the great sword Retaliator, the sword of his father, from his belt and place the point against Sreng's breast and drive that point deep into the Fhoi Myore's corrupting heart so that Sreng let forth a yell.

Sreng's last yell frightened Corum more than any of the previous events had done. For Sreng's last yell had been a shout of pleasure, a wavering, delighted sound as Sreng found the death he had longed for.

Ilbrec stepped back from the Fhoi Myore body.

'Corum? Are you safe?'

'Safe enough, thanks to you, Ilbrec. I am bruised, that is all.'

'Thank yourself. What you did against Sreng was valiant. You have brains and great courage, Vadhagh. You saved yourself, for I should not have come in time otherwise.'

'Calatin,' said Corum. 'Where is he?'

'Fled. There is nothing we can do at present, for it becomes urgent to leave this place.'

'Why did Calatin want my body from Sreng?'

'Is that what he asked?' Ilbrec drew Corum up in the crook of his huge arm while he sheathed the sword Retaliator. 'I have no idea. I know nothing of Mabden needs.'

Ilbrec returned to the beach where the black horse Splendid

Mane cropped at the grass of the cliff, its pearl harness sparkling in the light of the moon which had now risen in the sky.

Corum saw a dark shape lying upon the beach.

'Goffanon?' he said. 'You were forced to slay him?'

'He showed every intention of slaying me,' said Ilbrec. 'I remembered what he told me of Calatin's enchantment. I suppose Calatin followed us and came close enough to Goffanon to re-exert his sorcerous influence. Poor Goffanon.'

'Should we bury him here?' said Corum. He was full of misery, only now realizing the strength of his affection for the Sidhi smith. 'I would not like the Fhoi Myore to find him. Neither would I care for Calatin to – to make use of the body.'

'I agree that that would not be good,' said Ilbrec. 'But I think it unwise to bury him, you know.' He placed Corum again upon the saddle of Splendid Mane and he crossed to where Goffanon's body lay, heaving it up with some difficulty by placing Goffanon's limp arm around his neck and carrying the dwarf upon his back. 'He is a very heavy dwarf,' Ilbrec said.

Corum was distressed by Ilbrec's lightness of tone. But perhaps the giant simply hid his melancholy well.

'Then what shall we do?'

'Take him with us, I think, to Caer Mahlod.' Ilbrec put his foot in his stirrup and prepared to mount. He grunted and cursed as he got into the saddle after several attempts. 'Ach! The dwarf has bruised me all over. Damn him!' Then he smiled in his golden beard as he looked down and saw the expression upon Corum's face. 'Do not grieve, yet, for Goffanon the smith. Sidhi dwarfs are very hard to slay. This one, for instance, has merely had his silly senses knocked from him for a while.'

Ilbrec leaned back in his saddle, letting Splendid Mane take some of the weight of the dwarf. He held Goffanon's war-axe in the same hand which held the reins, resting it behind Corum across his saddle. 'Well, Splendid Mane, you carry three with you. I hope that you have lost none of your old skills.'

Corum's face broke into a smile. 'So he lives! Yet still we shall have to move swiftly to escape Calatin's power. And our boat was abandoned out there. How shall we cross the water?'

'Splendid Mane knows certain paths,' said Ilberc. 'Paths not quite of this dimension, if you understand me. Now, horse of my father, gallop. And gallop straight. Find the pathways through the sea.'

Splendid Mane snorted, lifted himself on his hind-legs for a moment, and plunged towards the sea.

Ilbrec laughed in delight, then, at Corum's considerable astonishment, as Splendid Mane's hooves touched the sea but did not sink.

Soon they were galloping out over the ocean, over the surface, beneath a huge moon which made the water shine, galloping for Caer Mahlod, galloping along the road across the water.

'You understand much concerning the Fifteen Realms, Vadhagh,' said Ilbrec as they rode, 'so you will understand that it is Splendid Mane's great talent to find certain veins, as it were, which do not belong exactly in this Realm, just as my sea-caverns do not belong. These veins can be found most particularly upon the surface of the sea and sometimes in the air itself. A Mabden would marvel and call such abilities sorcery, but we know otherwise. They make, however, a good spectacle when one wishes to impress the poor Mabden.'

And Ilbrec laughed again as Splendid Mane galloped on. 'We shall be in Caer Mahlod before morning!'

2. THE PLACE
OF POWER

The folk of the Tuha-na-Cremm Croich looked with awe upon the three as they approached the conical mound on which Caer Mahlod was built.

Goffanon was awake now and striding beside Splendid Mane. He grumbled of the bruises Ilbrec had inflicted, but his tone was good-humoured for he knew that Ilbrec had in reality saved both his life and his pride.

'So this is Caer Mahlod,' said the golden-haired son of Manannan as he brought Splendid Mane to a halt beside the water-ditch which now protected the citadel. 'It has changed little.'

'You have been here before?' asked Corum curiously.

'Indeed. In the old days there was a place near here where the Sidhi would gather. I remember being brought here by my father shortly before he went off to fight in the battle which took his life.'

Ilbrec dismounted and gently lifted Corum from the saddle to place him upon the ground. Corum was weary, for they had ridden all night over those strange, other-realm pathways across the sea; but he still kept the casket, the gift of King Daffyn and his daughter-in-law, tightly under his arm. His mail coat was torn and his helmet was much-dented. The sword at his side was notched and blunted; he bore the signs of many small wounds, and when he walked it was painfully and slowly. But

118

there was pride, too, in his bearing as he called for the draw-bridge to be lowered:

'It is Corum come back to Caer Mahlod,' he cried, 'bringing two friends, allies of the Mabden.' He lifted the casket in his two hands, the one of flesh and the other of silver. 'And, see, here are the Oak of Gold and the Ram of Silver which will give you back your High King.'

The bridge was lowered and on the other side waited Medhbh of the Long Arm and Jhary-a-Conel with his cat upon his shoulder and his hat upon his head. Medhbh ran forward to embrace Corum, kissing his bruised face, taking off his helmet and stroking his hair.

'My love,' she said. 'My elven love, come home.' And she was weeping.

Jhary-a-Conel said soberly:

'Amergin is close to death. A few more hours and he will bleat his last, I fear.'

Grave-faced Mannach appeared. With dignity he welcomed the two Sidhi.

'We are much honoured. Corum brings fine, good friends to Caer Mahlod.'

Looking about the morning streets at the people who were beginning to gather, Corum saw none of King Fiachadh's people.

'Has King Fiachadh gone?'

'He had to leave, for there were rumours that the Fhoi Myore marched over an ice-bridge to attack his land.'

'The Fhoi Myore marched,' said Corum, 'and they made an ice-bridge over the sea right enough, but it was not King Fiachadh's folk they attacked. They went to Caer Garanhir and there we fought them, Goffanon, Ilbrec and I.' And he told King Mannach of all that had befallen him since he and Goffanon had parted from Jhary-a-Conel.

'But now,' he ended, 'I would eat, for I am famished, and doubtless my friends are hungry, too. And I would rest for an hour or two, since we have ridden through the whole night to be here.'

'You slew a Fhoi Myore!' said Medhbh. 'So they can be slain by others than the Black Bull?'

'I helped slay one – a very minor one, a very ill one,' smiled Corum. 'But if it had not been for Ilbrec here, I should now be crushed beneath the monster.'

'I owe you much, great Ilbrec,' said Medhbh, bowing her

head to the Sidhi. Her thick, red hair fell down over her face and she brushed it back as she tilted back her head to look up into the smiling eyes of the giant Sidhi. 'I should be mourning now if it were not for you.'

'He's brave, this tittle Vadhagh.' The golden-bearded youth laughed, seating himself casually upon the flat roof of a nearby house.

'He is brave,' agreed Medbhb.

'But come,' King Mannach said urgently, taking Corum's arm, 'you must see Amergin and tell me what you think of his condition.' King Mannach looked up at Ilbrec. 'I fear you could not enter our low doors, Lord Sidhi.'

'I'll wait here cheerfully until I'm needed,' said Ilbrec. 'But you go, Goffanon, if that is fitting.'

Goffanon said: 'I should like to see what has happened to the Archdruid, we took so much trouble saving him.' He left his axe standing near Ilbrec's right foot and followed after King Mannach, Medhbh, Jhary-a-Conel and Corum as they entered the king's hall and crossed it, waiting while King Mannach opened a door and led them inside.

The room was lit brightly with brands. No attempt had been made to remove Amergin's sheepskin clothing, but it had been cleaned. The High King lay beside a number of plates on which various kinds of grasses had been laid.

'We sought desperately to discover which would sustain him best, but none of them have done more than prolong his life by a few hours,' King Mannach said. He opened the casket Corum had handed him. He frowned as he inspected the two beautifully made images. 'How are these to be used?'

Corum shook his head. 'I know not.'

'He did not tell us,' Jhary-a-Conel said.

'Then has your quest been fruitless?' Medhbh asked.

'I think not,' said Goffanon, stepping forward. 'I know something of the properties of the Oak and the Ram. There was a legend amongst our folk that they had been fashioned for a particular purpose, when the Mabden race would be in great danger and few Sidhi to help them in their struggles. I recall that there was a Sidhi called Oak Woman who gave a pledge to the Mabden, but the nature of that pledge I do not know. We must take the Oak and the Ram to a place of power, perhaps to Craig Dôn . . . '

'It would be too far to journey,' Corum said reasonably. 'Look – life flees Amergin even as we speak.'

'It is true,' said Medhbh. The High King's breath was shallow and his flesh as pale as his woollen garments. His face looked old and lined whereas previously, perhaps because he was untroubled in his guise of a sheep, it had seemed young.

'Cremmsmound,' said Jhary-a-Conel. 'That is a place of power.'

'Aye,' said King Mannach with a faint smile. 'It is. At Cremmsmound we summoned you, Prince Corum, to come to our aid.'

'Then perhaps there we can release the magic of the Oak and the Ram,' Goffanon said, frowning and tugging at his matted black beard. 'Could you ask Amergin, Jhary-a-Conel, if Cremmsmound is a good place?'

But Jhary shook his head. 'My cat reports that the Archdruid is too weak. To speak with him now would be to shock what remains of his life from him.'

'This is an irony I do not like,' said King Mannach. 'To be defeated now, after so many deeds of courage have been performed.'

And, as if in agreement with the king, there came from the figure on the floor a faint, melancholy bleat.

His body trembling with sudden emotion, King Mannach turned away. He groaned. 'Our High King! Our High King!'

Goffanon laid a huge, gnarled hand upon Mannach's shoulder. 'Let us take him, anyway, to Cremmsmound, to that place of power. Who knows what will happen? Tonight the moon shall be at its fullest and will shine upon the mistletoe and the oaks. It is an excellent night for the working of incantations and charms, I am told, for the fullness of the moon indicates when the Fifteen Planes intersect most closely.'

'Is that why folk regard the full moon as having particular properties?' Medhbh had been told something of the Realms beyond the Earth by Corum. 'It is not simply superstition?'

'The moon itself has no power,' said Goffanon. 'It is merely, in this case, a measuring instrument. It tells us, roughly, how the different planes of the Earth move in relation to each other.'

'Strange,' said King Mannach, 'how we are inclined to reject such knowledge simply because it becomes corrupted by primitive minds. A year ago I should not have believed in the legends of the Sidhi, in the legends of Cremm Croich, in the folktales of our people or in any of our old superstitions. And in a way I would have been right, for there are those who have an interest in using legends and superstitions for their own ends.

121

They cherish such notions not for their own sake but for the use to which they can be put. Poor, wretched people who cannot love life seek for something beyond life, something they prefer to regard as better than life. And, as a result, they corrupt the knowledge they discover and, in turn, associate their own weaknesses with this knowledge – at least, in the minds of others, like myself.

'But the knowledge you have brought us, Corum – that extends our appreciation of life. You speak of a variety of worlds where mankind flourishes. You offer us information which brings light to our understanding, where the corrupt and the lost speak only of mysteries and dark superiorities and seek to elevate themselves in their own eyes and the eyes of their fellows.'

'I follow you,' said Corum, for he had some experience himself of what King Mannach meant. 'Yet even when the minds are primitive and the knowledge corrupt, this can spawn a huge and ugly power of its own. And can the power of Light exist without the presence of the power of Dark? Can generosity survive without greed or ignorance survive without knowledge?'

'That is ever the puzzle of the Mabden dream,' said Jhary-a-Conel, almost to himself, 'and that, doubtless, is why I am encouraged to remain in that dream wherever, in all the Fifteen Realms and beyond, it manifests itself.' Then he spoke more briskly: 'But this particular dream will fade very soon unless we find a means of reviving Amergin. Come, let us bear him swiftly to this place of power, this Cremmsmound.'

And it was only as they prepared to leave for the mound in the oak grove that Corum realized he had a profound reluctance to accompany them.

He realized that he feared Cremmsmound, for all that it was the place he had first seen when King Mannach and his folk called him from their past, from Castle Erorn and his brooding and his memories of Rhalina.

Corum mocked himself, realizing that he was both tired and hungry and that when he had rested a little and eaten a little and spent a little time in the company of his lovely Medhbh he would no longer experience such silly feelings.

Yet they remained with him until the evening when King Mannach, Medhbh of the Long Arm, Jhary-a-Conel, Goffanon the dwarf, Ilbrec of the Sidhi riding on Splendid Mane, Corum and all King Mannach's folk from the fortress city of Caer Mahlod, took the near-dead body of the High King Amergin forth and bore it towards the forest where, in a glade, rose the mound under which, according to legend, Corum – or a previous incarnation of Corum – had been buried.

A little faint sunlight lingered among the great trees of the forest, creating dark and mysterious shadows which seemed to Corum to contain more than rhododendrons and brambles, more than squirrels or foxes or birds.

Twice he shook his head, cursing his own weariness for putting stupid notions into his mind.

And then at last the party reached Cremmsmound in the oak glade.

They reached the place of power.

3. THE GOLDEN OAK
AND
THE SILVERN RAM

For a moment, as he entered the oak grove, Corum felt a cold enter his body which was even more profound than that which he had experienced at Caer Llud and he felt that this was the coldness of death.

He began to remember the prophecy of Ieveen the Seeress whom he had met on the way to Hy-Breasail. She had told him to fear a harp – well, he did fear a harp. She had told him to fear a brother, too. Did his 'brother' rest under the grass-mound in the oak grove, under the artificial hill surrounded by oaks of all ages, the holy place of the folk of Caer Mahlod? Was there another Corum – the real hero Cremm, perhaps – who would rise from the earth to slay him for his presumption?

Was it Cremm he had seen in his dream while he slept at Craig Dôn?

The mount was a silhouette against the sinking sun and the moon was already rising. A hundred faces turned upwards to look at the moon, but these were not the faces of superstitious men and women. Each face reflected a curiosity and a sense of impending wonderment. It was quiet in the oak grove as they stood in a circle about the mound.

Then Ilbrec lifted the puny body of the High King in his great arms and Ilbrec walked up the mound and placed the High King at the very top. And then Ilbrec, too, turned his face up to look at the moon.

Ilbrec walked slowly back down the mound to stand beside his old friend Goffanon.

Next came King Mannach to the mound, walking slowly up and holding the open casket in his arms. From within the casket gleamed gold and silver. King Mannach placed the golden oak at Amergin's head, where it faced the fading sun, and the oak shone brightly, seeming to absorb all the remaining rays. And King Mannach placed the image of the silver ram at Amergin's feet so that the rays of the moon would fall upon it, and already the silver ram burned white and cold.

Corum thought that, save for their size, those two images could be a living tree and a living ram, so fine was their workmanship. The gathering pressed closer around the mound as King Mannach descended, all eyes upon the prone body of the High King and the oak and the ram. Only Corum hung back. The cold had gone from his body, yet he still shivered, still fought the fear which sought to fill his mind.

Then came Goffanon the smith, his double-bladed axe, which he had forged himself centuries before, upon his broad shoulder, the gold of the oak and the silver of the ram reflected in his helm, greaves and breastplate of polished iron. And Goffanon walked half-way up the mound and paused, lowering his axe so that the blade rested upon the turf and his hands rested upon the shaft.

Corum smelled the rich and subtle scents of the trees, the brambles, the rhododendrons and the grass of the forest. Those scents were warm and good and should have lulled the sense of fear in Corum, but they did not. Still he did not join the throng, but remained at the edge of the gathering wishing that Medhbh had not pressed forward with the rest, wishing that she stood beside him to comfort him. But none knew what Corum felt. All eyes were upon the figure of the High King, upon the image of the oak at his head and the image of the ram at his feet. And Corum became conscious of a silence descending upon the forest; there was neither the sound of animals nor the rustle of leaves. There was a stillness as if nature itself waited to learn what events would now come to pass.

And Goffanon lifted his huge and bearded head towards the moon and he began to sing in the clear, deep voice which had earlier sounded his own death-song, when he thought that the Brothers to the Pines would slay him. And though the words were spoken in the Sidhi tongue, which was related to the tongues of the Vadhagh and the Mabden, Corum heard many of them and understood them.

Ancient were the Sidhi
    Ere before the Calling,
They died abroad
    In noble circumstance,

Binding vows they made,
    Stronger than blood,
Greater than love,
    To aid the Mabden race,

In clouds they came
    To the Islands of the West,
Their weapons and their music
    In their arms,

Gloriously they fought,
    And nobly died
In battle and in grief,
    Honouring their vows,

Ancient were the Sidhi,
    Proud in word and deed;
Ravens followed them
    In alien realms.

Ancient were the Sidhi!
    E'en in death
They swore the fulfilment
    Of all oaths,

Chariots and treasures,
    Mounds and caverns,
Are their monuments,
    And their names,

Of these heroes few remain
    To guard against the Pines,
The oaks are dying.
    Unearthly winter slays them,

Ancient were the Sidhi,
*   Brothers to the Oak,*
Friends of the Sun,
*   Enemies of the Ice.*

The ravens grew fat
*   On Sidhi flesh.*
Who is there now
*   To aid the Oak?*

Once Oak Woman stood amongst us,
*   Sharing her strength;*
Her knowledge brought us courage
*   And the Fhoi Myore fell.*

The Fhoi Myore fell.
*   Sunlight swept the West,*
And Oak Woman slept.
*   Her work was done.*

Ancient were the Sidhi!
*   Few there were who lived.*
Prophetic voices spoke,
*   But the Sidhi would not hear.*

Oak Woman stirred,
*   Pledges she made.*
If cold returned,
*   She would wake.*

Mystic talismans
*   She fashioned,*
Against the Winter's might;
*   To save her Oaks.*

Sleeping, Oak Woman smiled,
*   Safe against the snow,*
Her oath ensured,
*   Her word made strong.*

In nine fights the Fhoi Myore fell;
*   In nine fights died the Sidhi;*

Few heroes left the final field.
  Manannan died and all his throng.

Dying, great Manannan knew peace.
  In vain he had not fought,
For he recalled Oak Woman's vow
  To aid tomorrow's race.

Oak Woman slept in sanctuary.
  A word would wake her.
The tenth great fight grew near.
  The word was sought.

The word was lost.
  Three heroes sought it.
Goffanon sang a song.
  The word was found.

None moved as Goffanon's song ended. The Sidhi smith lowered his head and rested his head upon his chin, waiting.

From the prone figure who lay upon the crown of the mound there came a small, weak sound, at first little more than the familiar, tragic bleating.

Goffanon raised his head, listening carefully. The note of the bleating changed for a brief instant and then faded.

Goffanon turned to face those who waited.

He spoke in a low, tired voice. He said:

'The word is "Dagdagh".'

And as he heard the word Corum gasped, for an awful shock ran through his whole body and made him stagger, made his heart pound and his head swim, though the word meant nothing to his conscious mind. He saw Jhary-a-Conel turn, white-faced, and stare at him.

And then the harp began to play.

Corum had heard the harp before. It was the harp which had sounded from Castle Erorn when he had first come to Caer Mahlod. It was the harp he had heard in dreams. Now only the tune was different. This tune was rousing and triumphant; a tune of bounding confidence, a laughing tune.

He heard Ilbrec whisper in astonishment: 'The Dagdagh harp! I thought it stilled forever.'

Corum felt that he drowned. He drew great gulps of air into his lungs as he sought to control his terror. He looked fearfully behind him amongst the dark trees, but he saw nothing save the shadows.

And when he looked back at the mound he was half-blinded, for the Golden Oak was growing, its golden branches spreading over the heads of those who watched and emitting a marvellous radiance. And Corum's fear was forgotten in his wonderment. Still the Golden Oak grew until it seemed to cover the whole mound and Amergin's body could just be discerned beneath it.

And all who watched were transfixed as from the oak there stepped a maiden as tall as Ilbrec himself; a woman whose hair was the green of oak-leaves and whose garment was the deep brown of an oak's trunk and whose skin was as pale as the flesh of the oak which lies beneath the bark. And she was Oak Woman, smiling and speaking:

'I recall my pledge. I recall the prophecy. I know you, Goffanon, but I do not know these others.'

'They are Mabden, save for Corum and Ilbrec. They are a good folk, Oak Woman, and they revere the oaks. See, oaks grow all around, for this is their Place of Power, their Holy Place.' Goffanon spoke almost hesitantly, seeming as impressed by this vision as were the Mabden. 'Ilbrec is your friend's son, Manannan's son. Of the Sidhi only he and I remain. And Corum is our kinsman, of the Vadhagh race. The Fhoi Myore have returned and we fight them, but we are weak. Amergin, High King of the Mabden, lies at your feet, enchanted. His soul has become the soul of a sheep and we cannot find the soul he lost.'

'I will find his soul,' said Oak Woman, smiling slightly, 'if that is your need.'

'It is, Oak Woman.'

The Oak Woman looked down upon Amergin. She bent and listened to his heart, then listened near his lips.

'His body dies,' she said.

There was a groan from all who watched save Corum and Corum was listening for the sound of the terrible harp, but it sounded no longer.

Then Oak Woman took the Silvern Ram from Amergin's feet.

'This was the prophecy,' she said, 'that the Ram must be given a soul. Now the soul of Amergin begins to leave his body and provides a soul for the Ram. Amergin must die.'

'No!' a score of lips shouted the word.

129

'But you must wait,' said Oak Woman chidingly with a smile.
She placed the ram at Amergin's head, crying:

> Soul speeding to the Mother Sea;
>   Lamb bleating at the rising moon;
> Pause soul, silence lamb!
>   Here is your home!

Now the bleating began afresh, but this time it was a lusty
bleating, the bleating of a new-born lamb. And the voice came
from the Silvern Ram as the moonlight fell upon its silver fleece
and even as they watched they saw it grow and the bleating
grew deeper and turned to a deep, lowing sound and the Silvern
Ram turned its head and its eyes had the same intelligence
which Corum had witnessed in the eyes of the Black Bull of
Crinanass and he knew then that this animal, like the Bull, was
one of a flock which the Sidhi had brought with them when
they came to this Realm. The Ram saw the Oak Woman and it
ran to her and nuzzled her hand.

Then Oak Woman smiled again, turning her head towards the
sky, calling:

> Soul dwelling in the Mother Sea,
>   Leave your tranquil haven.
> Your earthly destiny is yet unfinished.
>   Here is your home!

And the body of the High King stirred as if in sleep. And
the hands crept to the face and the eyes opened and upon those
blank features there was now written an expression of peace and
wisdom and where age had lined the flesh there was now youth
and where the limbs had been feeble there was now strength.
And a cool, well-timbred voice said with faint astonishment:

'I am Amergin.'

Then the Archdruid rose up, tearing off the sheepskin hood
and releasing his fair hair so that it fell upon his shoulders.
And he ripped the sheepskin clothing from his body to reveal
a form that was naked and beautiful and clad only in bracelets
of hammered red gold.

And now Corum knew why the folk had mourned for their
High King, for Amergin radiated both humility and dignity,
wisdom and humanity.

130

'Yes,' he said, touching his breast and speaking wonderingly, 'I am Amergin.'

Now a hundred swords flashed in the moonlight as the Mabden saluted their Archdruid.

'Hail, Amergin! Hail, Amergin of the family of Amergin!'

And many men were there who wept for joy and embraced each other, and even the Sidhi, Goffanon and Ilbrec, raised their weapons in salute to Amergin.

The Oak Woman lifted her hand and she pointed a white finger through the throng to where Corum stood, still full of fear and unable to join the others in their joy.

'You are Corum,' said Oak Woman. 'You saved the High King and you found the oak and the ram. You are the Mabden champion now.'

'So I am told,' said Corum in a small, tortured voice.

'You shall be great in the memories of this folk,' said Oak Woman, 'yet you shall know little lasting happiness here.'

'I understand that also,' said Corum, and he sighed.

'Your destiny is a noble one,' continued Oak Woman, 'and I thank you for your dedication to that destiny. You have saved the High King and enabled me to keep my word.'

'You have slept all this time in the Golden Oak?' said Corum. 'You have waited for this day?'

'I have slept and I have waited.'

'But what power kept you upon this plain?' he asked, for this question had been puzzling him ever since Oak Woman had appeared. 'What great power was it, Oak Woman?'

'The power of my pledge,' she said.

'Naught else?'

'Why should aught else be necessary?'

And then the Oak Woman stepped back into the trunk of the Golden Oak and was followed by the Silvern Ram and the light from the oak began to fade and then the outlines of the oak itself began to fade and then the Golden Oak, the Silvern Ram and Oak Woman were gone and were never afterward seen again in mortal lands.

4. THE DAGDAGH HARP

Now the folk of Caer Mahlod carried their High King Amergin joyfully back to their fortress city and many danced as they moved through the moonlit forest and there were broad grins upon the faces of Goffanon and Ilbrec, who was mounted on his black horse Splendid Mane.

And only Corum's brow was clouded, for he had heard words from Oak Woman which were less than cheering, and he lagged behind and was late in entering the king's hall.

Their own good spirits clouding their vision, none of the others saw that Corum did not smile, and they slapped him upon his shoulders and they toasted him and they honoured him as much as they honoured their own High King.

And the feasting began, and the drinking, and the singing to the sound of the Mabden harps.

So Corum, seated beside Medhbh on one side and King Mannach on the other, drank a considerable amount of sweet mead and tried to drive the memory of the harp from his mind.

He saw King Mannach lean across to where Goffanon was seated next to Ilbrec (who was manfully showing no discomfort as he sat cramped and cross-legged beside the bench) and ask: 'How knew you the incantation which raised the Oak Woman, Sir Goffanon?'

'I knew no special incantation,' said Goffanon, lifting a cauldron of mead from his lips and setting it upon the table. 'I trusted to my hidden memories and the memories of my people. I hardly heard the words of the song myself. They came almost unbidden from my lips. I relied upon this to reach both the Oak Woman and Amergin's spirit wherever it drifted. It was Amergin himself who gave me the word which in turn produced that music which, in its turn, began the transformation.'

'Dagdagh,' said Medhbh, unaware that Corum shuddered at the sound. 'An old word. A name, perhaps?'

'A title, also. A word of many meanings.'

'A Sidhi name?'

'I think not – though it is associated with the Sidhi. The Dagdagh led the Sidhi into battle on more than one occasion. I am young, you see, as the Sidhi measure age, and I took part in only two of the nine historic fights against the Fhoi Myore and by that time the name of the Dagdagh was no longer spoken. I know not why, save that there was a hint that Dagdagh had betrayed our cause.'

'Betrayed it? Not this night, surely?'

'No,' said Goffanon, his brow darkening a trifle. 'Not this night.' And he raised the cauldron to his lips and took a thoughtful swig.

Jhary-a-Conel left his seat and came to stand behind Corum. 'Why so pensive, old friend?'

Corum was grateful that Jhary had noticed his mood and at the same time did not wish to spoil Jhary's celebration. He smiled as best he could and shook his head:

'Weariness, I suppose. I've slept little of late.'

'That harp,' continued Medhbh and Corum wished that she would stop. 'I recall hearing a similar harp.' She turned to Corum. 'At Castle Owyn when we rode there once.'

'Aye,' he murmured. 'At Castle Owyn.'

'A mysterious harp,' said King Mannach, 'but I for one am grateful to it and would hear its music again if it brings us such gifts as the restoration of our High King,' and he raised his mead-horn to toast Amergin who sat smiling and calm, but drinking little, at the head of the table.

'Now we shall mass,' said King Mannach, 'all the folk of the Mabden who remain. We shall build a great army and we shall ride against the Fhoi Myore. And this time we shall leave none alive!'

'Brave words,' said Ilbrec, 'but we need more than courage. We need weapons such as my sword Retaliator. We need cunning – aye, and caution where it suits our cause.'

'You speak wisely, Sir Sidhi,' said Amergin. 'You echo my own thoughts.' His old and yet youthful face was full of good humour as if he were not troubled one bit by the great problem of the Fhoi Myore. He wore a robe, now, of loose yellow samite bordered with designs of blue and red and his hair was braided and lay upon his back.

'With Amergin to counsel us and Corum to lead us into war,' said King Mannach, 'I believe that I am not foolish to show some optimism.' He smiled at Corum. 'We grow stronger. Not long since our lives seemed lost and our race destroyed, but now ... '

'Now,' said Corum finishing a whole horn of mead and wiping his lips upon the back of his silver hand, 'now we celebrate great victories.' Unable to control himself he rose from the bench, stepped over it, and strode from the hall.

He walked into the night, through the streets of Caer Mahlod – streets which were filled with merry-makers, with music and with laughter – and he went through the gate and over the turf towards where the distant sea boomed.

And at last he stood alone upon the brink of the chasm which separated him from the ruins of his old home, Castle Erorn, which this folk called Castle Owyn and thought a formation of natural rock.

In the moonlight the ruins glowed and Corum wished that he could fly across the gulf and enter Castle Erorn and find a gateway back to his own world. There he had been lonely, but that was not the loneliness he felt now. Now he had a sense of complete desolation.

And then he saw a face staring back at him from out of the broken windows of the castle. It was a handsome face, a face with a skin of gold; a mocking face.

Corum called hoarsely:

'Dagdagh! Is it Dagdagh?'

And he heard laughter which became the music of a harp.

Corum drew his sword. Below him the sea foamed and leapt on the rocks at the foot of the cliff. He prepared to leap the gulf, to seek out the youth with the skin of gold, to demand why the youth plagued him so. He poised himself, caring not if he fell and died.

And then he felt a soft, strong hand upon his shoulder. He tried to shake it free, still crying:

'Dagdagh! Let me be!'

Medhbh's voice said close to his ear, 'Dagdagh is our friend,

134

Corum. Dagdagh saved our High King.'

Corum turned towards her and saw her troubled eyes staring into his single eye.

'Put away your sword,' she said. 'There is no one there.'

'Did you not hear the music of his harp?'

'I heard the wind making music in the crannies of Castle Owyn. That is what I heard.'

'You did not see his face, his mocking face?'

'I saw a cloud move across the moon,' she said. 'Come back now, Corum, to our celebrations.'

And he sheathed his sword and he sighed and he let her lead him back to Caer Mahlod.

EPILOGUE

And that was the end of the Tale of the Oak and the Ram.

Messengers went across the sea, taking the news to all: The High King was restored to his folk. They sailed to the west to tell King Fiachadh of the Tuha-na-Manannan (named for Ilbrec's own family, Corum now knew) and they sailed to the north where the Tuha-na-Tir-nam-Beo were told the news. And they told the Tuha-na-Anu and they told King Daffyn of the Tuha-na-Gwyddneu Garanhir. And wherever they found Mabden tribes they told them that the High King dwelled at Caer Mahlod, that Amergin debated the question of war against the Fhoi Myore and that the representatives of all the tribes of the Mabden race were called there to plan the last great fight which would decide who ruled the Islands of the West.

In the smithies there was a clanging and roaring as swords were fashioned, and axes made and spears honed under the direction of that greatest of all smiths, Goffanon.

And there was excitement and optimism in the homes of the Mabden as they wondered what Corum of the Silver Hand and Amergin the Archdruid would decide and where the battle would take place and when it would begin.

And the others listened to Ilbrec who would sit in the fields and tell them the tales he had heard from his father, whom many thought to be the greatest of the Sidhi heroes, tales of the Nine Fights against the Fhoi Myore and the deeds which were done. And they were heartened by these tales (some of which they knew) and glad to understand that the heroism which had been thought to be the fanciful invention of bards had actually taken place.

And only when they saw Corum, pale and pensive, his head bent as if he listened for a voice he could not quite hear, did they consider the tragedy of those tales, of the great hearts which had been stilled in the service of their race.

And at those times did the folk of Caer Mahlod become thoughtful and at those times they understood the enormity of the sacrifice made for their cause by the Vadhagh Prince called Corum of the Silver Hand.

THIS ENDS THE SECOND VOLUME OF THE CHRONICLE OF CORUM AND THE SILVER HAND

MICHAEL MOORCOCK

'Like Tolkein and Roger Zalazny, Moorcock has the ability to create a wholly imaginative world landscaped with vivid and sometimes frightening reality, and peopled with magicians, heroes and monsters who are far from the one dimensional creatures of fairy tales but who possess human warmth and interaction . . . bargains, symbols, rituals and vicious battles enliven a glittering story as Corum embarks on another heroic quest' – *The Times*

'One of the best fantasy writers in the language' – *Tribune*

Other titles by Michael Moorcock available in Quartet paperback editions are –

THE ENGLISH ASSASSIN – A Romance of Entropy featuring Jerry Cornelius.

THE WAR LORD OF THE AIR – A Captain Bastable adventure.

THE SLEEPING SORCERESS – An Elric story.

THE BULL AND THE SPEAR – the first volume of The Chronicle of the Prince Corum and the Silver Hand trilogy.

Soon to be available –

THE SWORD AND THE STALLION – the third volume of the Chronicle of the Prince Corum and the Silver Hand trilogy.

THE LAND LEVIATHAN – A new Captain Bastable story.

These books are obtainable from booksellers and newsagents or can be ordered direct from the publishers. Send a cheque/ postal order for the purchase price plus 6p postage and packing to Quartet Books Limited, PO Box 11, Falmouth, Cornwall TR10 9EN